D0782671

SHOWDOWN AT VIKING CAVE

G·K
Hall
&Co.

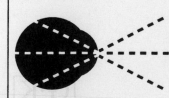

SHOWDOWN AT VIKING CAVE

W
BLAIR

Clifford Blair

G.K. Hall & Co.
Thorndike, Maine

Published in 1994 by arrangement with Walker Publishing
Company, Inc.

All the characters and events protrayed in this work are fictitious.

G.K. Hall Large Print Paperback Collection.

The text of this Large Print edition is unabridged.
Other aspects of the book may vary from the original edition.

Set in 16 pt. News Plantin by Warren Doersam.

Printed in the United States on acid-free paper.

Library of Congress Cataloging in Publication Data

Blair, Clifford.
    Showdown at Viking Cave / Clifford Blair.
       p.   cm.
    ISBN 0-8161-7473-3 (alk. paper : lg. print)
    1. Large type books. I Title.
  [PS3552.L3462S56 1994b]
  813′.54—dc20   94-27154

With love,
to Lucille McAnally,
my aunt
and
my friend.

CHAPTER 1

Wayne Saddler heard the clatter of hoofbeats outside the barn, and old habit made him reach automatically for the six-gun he still wore holstered at his side.

"Hello, the homestead!" a man's familiar voice called then, and Wayne let himself relax as a faint grin pulled at his mouth.

He left the plow horse in the traces and moved to the high double doorway of the barn. He squinted for a moment against the slanting rays of the late-afternoon sun. Three riders had reined up in front of the house, which stood opposite the barn. The three of them were looking about for signs of life.

It was the lean, graying rider, with a badge on his chest and two ivory-handled six-shooters on his belt, who spotted Wayne first. The laconic lawman wheeled his horse easily about and said, "Howdy, farmer."

"Deputy," Wayne drawled in response. The grin still tugged at his mouth. He and United States Deputy Marshal Heck Thomas went back a ways.

Heck had spent more than thirty years taming the trouble towns of the shrinking West, tracking down the wild breed of men who operated outside the law. Along with a handful of other deputies, he now rode herd on the tumultuous region of Oklahoma Territory. The law hadn't come easy to the Territory; Heck and his fellow peace officers had their hands full dealing with the outlaws, rustlers, and bandits who preyed on the townfolk and homesteaders who had come from all over the country to settle the newly opened lands.

Heck wore his customary knee-high boots, corduroy trousers, and flannel shirt. He sat his big gray with ease as he gestured at his companions. "I brought along a couple of folks who might have a proposition for you. This here's Professor Trevor Hastings, with his daughter and assistant, Miss Laura Hastings."

Wayne's attention had already been drawn to the pretty, dark-eyed young woman who seemed almost as comfortable astride her palomino as Heck did on his own mount. She wore a pair of men's jeans and work shirt, although they didn't conceal the womanly shape of her figure. A wealth of black hair, glinting in the sun, was pulled back in a practical ponytail beneath a flat-brimmed Stetson.

Without thinking about it, Wayne gave her a little courtly bow, as if he were back on the dance floor at a military ball. "My pleasure, miss."

She smiled graciously and inclined her head. Her horse shifted a little, so Wayne couldn't read her expression.

Reluctantly he switched his attention to her father. Trevor Hastings was a man who bore more the stamp of the outdoorsman than of the scholar.

8

Weathered and wiry, he too seemed at home on his mount. He wore khaki pants and shirt, a pistol in a snap holster on a wide belt, and what Wayne recognized as a pith helmet on his graying head. In all, he looked able enough, if a mite out of place here in the Territory.

"Professor." Wayne nodded in greeting. "Make yourselves to home at the house." Wayne waved in that direction. "I've been pushing a plow most of the day. Let me see to my horse, and I'll be along shortly."

"Good enough." Heck reined his gray around. "Professor, Miss Laura, this way."

Wayne thought he saw the young woman eyeing him as she turned her mare, but it was hard to tell because of the Stetson. He watched a moment as the three of them walked their horses toward the house. Then he returned to the barn.

Quickly he unhitched the plow horse and put him in the stall with a ration of oats. Later, he would put him out to pasture with his saddle stock. Conscious of the female company waiting at the house, he took time to work the handle of the pump over the water trough until a clear stream of well water was flowing. Then he cupped his hands beneath the water and doused his face, rinsed out his kerchief, and used it to scrub the day's accumulation of grit and dust from his face. The cool water felt good on his sun-scorched skin. This day in early spring already carried a hint of the coming summer heat.

Last, he ran his fingers through his tangled hair

and clamped his battered straw Stetson back in place. He wondered what sort of proposition Heck had in mind that had led him to bring such an odd pair out here to his homeplace.

He headed toward the house. It wasn't much more than a log cabin with a lean-to room he had added when he bought the place. The original owner had homesteaded this quarter-section in the Land Run but had gotten his fill of farming and headed back east. Simple though it was, the house was still a sight better than the soddies — dirt houses built from bricks of sod — that many families called home out here on the prairie.

As Wayne drew near, Heck's voice reached him through one of the windows. "Like I was telling you folks, Wayne's dad was in the army — served in the Indian Wars. He saw to it that Wayne went to West Point for an education. When he finished his schooling, Wayne served a hitch in the cavalry himself. Rode these parts on patrol before they were opened for settlement. He took a liking to the region and came back out here when his hitch was up."

The horses of the visitors were tethered in front of the cabin. Wayne noted a Winchester sheathed on the girl's saddle.

As he mounted the steps, he heard Heck say, "He served as a U.S. deputy marshal himself for a spell — a mighty good one, too. That's when I met up with him." A reflective note entered Heck's tone. "He and I rode some hard trails together. Anyway, he finally got the urge to settle

10

down, and went and bought this place. He's making a good go of it, too. He knows this region like a wolf knows its hunting grounds, so when I heard what you folks were after, I figured Wayne was just the man for you."

"Take all that with a grain of salt," Wayne advised as he entered the cabin.

The trio was seated at the table. Hastings eyed him curiously, but his daughter's expression was harder to fathom.

"Deputy Thomas says you were in the cavalry?"

"For a spell," he answered lamely. He didn't much like talking about himself. "And the name's Wayne," he added.

"Then I'm Laura," she responded quickly. "Is that saber one you carried in the cavalry?"

Wayne glanced where she indicated the gleaming sword and metal scabbard crossed over the fireplace. It was, he realized for the first time, the only bit of decoration in the cabin. "That's right," he told her.

The small front room suddenly seemed to close in on him. He felt big-footed and awkward in his own house. He could not remember the last time a woman had been in the cabin. "Let me offer you folks some vittles," he said to cover his unease. "It's getting on to suppertime, and I've got plenty." He moved toward the cookstove in the far corner.

"Oh, no!" Laura was on her feet in a trice. "I'll take care of that while you visit with Dad and Deputy Thomas." She was past him before he

11

could object. He caught a faint whiff of some flowery scent.

"Wood's there in the wood box," he offered.

"I'll do just fine," she assured him over her shoulder. "Don't concern yourself. But all three of you might want to step outside. I'm sure it'll get warm in here when I light the stove."

"Gentlemen, I suggest we take her advice," Hastings spoke up for the first time. Wayne could imagine his voice dominating a college lecture room. "My daughter usually has her way with things. She isn't one to trifle with."

"Hush, Dad," Laura admonished from in front of the stove. A flush had touched her cheeks.

The men went out onto the porch. Wayne still didn't have the foggiest notion what all this was about.

"I'll just let the professor give you the lowdown on what he's after," Heck said once they were seated at the table on the porch, under the shade of the cabin's eave.

Hastings cleared his throat. "I'm an archaeologist, Mr. Saddler," he began directly enough. "I study ancient peoples and their cultures and civilizations. In particular, I've made something of a specialty of the study of the seafaring peoples commonly known as the Vikings." He paused with lifted eyebrows, as though to gauge Wayne's familiarity with the term.

"Scandinavians," Wayne obliged him. "Mostly pirates and sea rovers. They raided all along the coasts of Europe back in the tenth century, if I recall my history correctly."

Hastings looked slightly abashed. "Yes, of course. The Vikings actually raided as early as the eighth century and as late as the eleventh. They were a remarkable people, and their influence on Europe was significant." Hastings paused before he continued. "It has long been my theory, based in part on certain evidence and artifacts I have uncovered in my research, that the Vikings were much greater seamen than has heretofore been suspected."

"Go on," Wayne prompted after a moment.

"It is my belief that the Vikings actually crossed the Atlantic Ocean and landed on this continent sometime in the tenth or eleventh century."

Wayne glanced at Heck. His face was as unreadable as a piece of leather. Plainly, though, he must have heard all this before. "I'm still listening," Wayne allowed.

"Naturally, I have a keen interest in finding proof to validate my theory. I'm currently associated with a university back east, which has had the foresight to provide some funding for me to carry out my research, although my views have proved rather controversial among certain of my peers."

"I can understand that," Wayne said dryly. "If you're right, quite a few history books might need to be rewritten."

"It would mean a monumental archaeological upheaval if I am proven correct," Hastings said. His eyes flashed with the passion of a scholar for his subject. "Naturally, I am always alert for news of finds that would serve to vindicate my theories. Most of my research has been focused on coastal areas where I deemed it most likely the Vikings would've left artifacts. So imagine my surprise when word reached me of a gigantic stone bearing what could well be Viking runes, located far from any coast."

"You're talking about Indian Rock," Wayne said with sudden understanding.

"Yes, exactly!" Hastings exclaimed. "Do you know of it?" He leaned forward intently across the table.

"Most folk hereabouts have heard of it," Wayne told him. "There's lots of tales about who engraved those characters, and what they mean. Fellow name of Luther Capp was probably the first white man to see it a few years back. He figured the carvings were the work of Indians, which is where the name comes from. But the tribes that are in this area say it was already here when the U.S. government moved them here. Whoever did the carving meant for it to last. And the stone itself is pretty impressive."

"Then you've seen it?" Hastings demanded.

"I ran across it while I was tracking a passel of owlhoots up on Poteau Mountain when I was wearing a deputy's badge. It's in a blind canyon partway up the mountain."

"How far is Poteau Mountain from here?"

Wayne gestured. "That's it over yonder."

Hastings turned eagerly to follow his pointing

14

finger. Even with dusk approaching, the dark shape of the small, rugged mount was clearly silhouetted where it rose up out of the rolling grassland some miles distant.

"The professor and his daughter came out here hoping to take a gander at Indian Rock," Heck Thomas interjected. "They were over to the town of Poteau looking for a guide, when I took a hand. Seems they'd gotten hitched up with Girt Tannery. He was offering to take them to see the Rock."

Wayne frowned. "Girt's bad medicine."

Heck nodded. "So I told them."

"Deputy Thomas was helpful enough to recommend you for the role of our guide." Hastings had pulled his eyes away from the brooding shape of the peak. "I wasn't too pleased with this man, Tannery, but he seemed to be the only person available."

"Likely no one else was willing to cross him and risk getting stomped or cut for their trouble," Wayne surmised wryly. He leaned back in his chair. "So, let me get the straight of this. You want me to guide you and your daughter up onto the mountain so you can take a look at Indian Rock. That's it?"

"I would welcome some time to study the rock and perhaps survey the area for other artifacts," Hastings elaborated. "Of course, we would be willing to pay you well for your time."

"How long are we talking about?"

"Possibly a week," Hastings answered cautiously. "Naturally, I would also pay to have some-

15

one look after your place here."

Wayne figured a month was more like the amount of time the professor would like to spend poking around up on the mountain. He nodded at the gun holstered on the belt Hastings wore. "What are you packing?"

"A Borchardt automatic pistol."

Wayne raised his eyebrows at the name of the rapid-firing European handgun. "Can you use it?"

"If need be. My research has taken me to many uncivilized regions. I've had to defend myself before."

"What about your daughter? Can she handle that Winchester on her saddle?"

"She has traveled with me since she was a child. She knows how to use firearms." Hastings eyed him shrewdly. "Are you anticipating trouble?"

Wayne shrugged. "Poteau Mountain's been the hideout for more than one gang of owlhoots. Parts of it are almost inaccessible. And there's plenty of loners and renegades — red and white alike — who hole up there now and again. Only a greenhorn would ride up that mountain and *not* expect trouble."

Hastings didn't seem fazed. "Very well. Deputy Thomas told me much the same thing. I understand the risk. With your capable presence, I am sure we will be able to deal with such problems if they arise. Well, Mr. Saddler, do we have a deal?"

Wayne chewed on it a little. The shadows were

lengthening across his homeplace. The tantalizing odors of cooking touched his nostrils. From inside the cabin came the faint sounds of Laura moving about and humming a pleasant tune.

The professor and his daughter might not be newborn calves venturing among hungry wolves, but they sure weren't any match for the breed of human predators they might run into on those remote slopes. And he could use the money. Trying to make a go of a one-man spread left plenty of loose ends that some extra cash might do to tie up. And, finally, he glanced at the lawman. Heck wanted him to do this, and the deputy wasn't a man to forget a favor.

The screen door to the cabin swung open, and Laura backed carefully onto the porch, a plate in either hand. She set one in front of Heck and the other before her father.

"Just a minute," she said with a quick smile at Wayne, "I'll get our plates next."

In moments she had hearty servings of fried ham, potatoes, greens, and corn dodgers for all of them, along with mugs of cool tea. Wayne felt her brush briefly against him as she set his mug beside his plate. He decided he liked the feeling of having her bustling about near him. When she finally seated herself across from him, he saw that her features were flushed with a warm radiance left by the heat from the cookstove.

Hastings offered a brief grace, then they fell to the meal. Laura was a good cook.

Even as he ate, Wayne sensed the others waiting

for his answer to their proposal. "What kind of evidence or artifacts are you hoping to find, Professor?" he asked between bites of ham.

"Possibly other runic carvings," Hastings answered eagerly. His eyes were alight again. "Traces of campsites, perhaps, or fragments of tools and weapons."

The sharp snap of Wayne's fingers cut off Hastings's list. "You folks excuse me," Wayne said as he rose. "I just remembered something you might be interested in seeing."

He ducked into the cabin. It took him only a moment to return with an item from the metal safekeeping box under his bunk.

"Would this be the sort of fragment you're looking to find?" he asked, placing a weathered piece of bronze on the table before Hastings.

Laura gasped. The professor's eyes widened. "By the saints," he murmured, and reached hesitantly for it. His eyes glowed.

Even Heck Thomas leaned forward for a better look. "A sword hilt."

Hastings picked up the hilt reverently, his gaze intense as he examined it.

All that remained of an ancient sword was the hilt, consisting of little more than a grip, a rounded pommel, and a short, down-curving crossguard. Whatever blade had once been afixed to it was long since gone. Wayne had no doubt that the weapon had been a formidable one. The hand that had gripped that hilt comfortably had to have been considerably larger than his own.

"Bronze," Hastings whispered. He squinted in the failing light, then traced his fingers gently over the dark metal, now green with age. "And I believe I can detect an engraving pattern even yet. Here, Laura, what do you think?" He passed the piece to her.

Wayne plucked a lantern from its customary nail near the door and lit it with a lucifer.

"Yes," she said softly, then repeated the word with more assurance, "Yes, I believe it is!" She looked to Wayne with wide eyes. "Wherever did you find it?"

"Plowed it up in one of my fields a while back. I could tell it was very old."

"It's Viking," Hastings stated as he reached to take the hilt from Laura. "Ninth or tenth century, almost certainly. Have you ever found anything else of this nature?"

"An occasional arrowhead. Nothing that old."

Hastings slowly shook his head in wonder, turning the hilt over and over in his hands. "I must have the opportunity to survey your land for other artifacts."

"Don't reckon that'll be any problem." Wayne found himself glancing at Laura. "You're welcome to take as long as you like when we get back from looking at Indian Rock."

Her face lit up. "Then, you'll take us?"

Wayne nodded. "I'll need a day or so to get things lined up here, make arrangements for somebody to look after my place. I'll meet you in the town of Heavener bright and early day after tomorrow. We'll pick up some supplies and head out."

Laura clapped her hands together. "Wonderful!"

After they finished eating Wayne walked his visitors out to their horses. Hastings thanked him for his hospitality and confirmed that he and Laura would meet Wayne in Heavener. "I'm even more eager than before to get to Indian Rock, Mr. Saddler," Hastings said politely.

As the professor and Laura mounted, Wayne looked into the distance at the vague, black shape of Poteau Mountain, somehow grim and foreboding in the gathering gloom. He remembered the dark tales about the mountain. Had Hastings heard any of those? He doubted it would make any difference in the professor's passion to go to the mountain to unearth its secrets.

"Girt Tannery was on the warpath when I pried him away from the professor and his daughter," Heck said quietly to Wayne before mounting up. "He's a bad man to cross. You be watching your backtrail, Wayne."

CHAPTER 2

As he rode into Heavener, Wayne eyed the half dozen or so horses at the hitch rail in front of the saloon. In the sharp light of the early-morning sun, the animals looked tired and miserable, as though they'd been in place for hours. Either their owners had come to town mighty early to get started drinking, or they had been in the saloon all night.

They were range horses, none of them familiar to him, which didn't mean much. Lots of folks of all kinds passed through Heavener these days. Located ten miles west of the Arkansas line and a couple of miles north of the Poteau River, Heavener had been built in Indian Territory to provide a depot for the junction of the KCS and the Arkansas Western railroads. It was the closest town to Poteau Mountain, which loomed off to the east.

A beam of sunlight glinted off something on the saddle of one of the horses in front of the saloon. Wayne reined in his paint a little closer. His squinted eyes widened a bit as he recognized the distinctive hilt and scabbard of a regulation cavalry saber lashed to the saddle alongside a sheathed long gun.

Not regular trappings for a cowpoke, he mused.

His hand moved automatically to his waist, where he used to carry his own saber when he wore the blue of the U.S. Cavalry. In its place was the hardwood hilt of a big false-edged bowie knife he'd slipped on his gunbelt that morning. He didn't wear it much these days, but in those years when he'd been packing a deputy's badge, it had been as much a part of him as his six-shooter, his Winchester, and the range gear he now wore. Like his saber, the bowie was something a man wore when he fancied trouble might be waiting a ways down the trail.

He glanced at the doorway of the saloon, and for a piece of a second he had a glimpse of a lean, cruel face. Wayne's nape prickled. It had been a spell since he'd laid eyes on Girt Tannery, but he was willing to bet that it was Girt's face he had just seen. Frowning, he kept an eye cocked over his shoulder until he was well past the saloon.

He rode on by one of the town's barbershops, beyond the Farmers and Merchants Bank and the publishing office of the *Heavener Globe*, then reined up in front of the general store. As he dismounted he cast one last searching look back at the saloon. The bored horses still stood hipshot and miserable. There was no sign of anyone watching him.

"You're here!" Laura Hastings exclaimed, emerging hurriedly from the store, her smile warm with welcome.

Wayne grinned and said, "Morning."

She took a couple more steps forward. She was

22

dressed in men's clothes as she had been two days earlier at his farm.

"We bought a pack mule like you suggested." She indicated a sturdy-looking animal tied next to their horses. "Dad's in the store checking on supplies. I'll tell him you're here."

Hastings emerged as if on cue. He also wore the same field gear Wayne had seen him in before. He greeted Wayne eagerly, then offered him a sheet of paper he held in one hand. "I took the liberty of making up a list of supplies — subject, of course, to your approval. They seem to have everything on the list in stock here. Take a look."

Wayne ran his eyes down the sheet. Hastings seemed to know what he was doing. The list contained all the basic grub and equipment needed for a stint in the wilderness.

"Can't add much to that," he admitted, passing the list back. "Do you have a rifle?"

"Why, yes, a four-sixteen double-bore Rigby with an ample supply of ammunition."

Wayne nodded his approval. What the heavy-caliber hunting rifle lacked in firing speed it more than made up for in stopping power. "Good weapon. What about Laura? Does she have a handgun?"

"No," she answered for herself. "But I can use a revolver, or an automatic like Dad carries."

"We'll get you fitted out with a six-shooter then," Wayne decided aloud. "Maybe a thirty-two caliber if the store's got any in stock. It won't hurt for each of us to have a sidearm as well as a saddle gun." Wayne gave another glance at the saloon as he spoke. He felt his muscles tense as the man he had glimpsed approached.

"Oh," Laura said softly as she followed the direction of his look, "it's Girt Tannery."

Wayne turned to face him. Lean and muscled as a mountain cougar, Girt wore filthy, tattered buckskins and knee-high Apache moccasins. A low-crowned Plainsman hat that had seen better days topped a shoulder-length mass of greasy blond hair. A revolver and a sheathed bowie knife rode at his waist. His thin face carried a half sneer, like the beginnings of a snarl.

Wayne stepped away from the professor and his daughter. Over Girt's shoulder he could see a handful of hard-looking men emerging from the saloon as though to watch a show. One of them at the forefront wore a long white duster. Wayne didn't waste too much time on them. Girt was the one to worry about just now.

"Mister Professor, Miss Laura, good morning to you." Girt spoke mockingly past Wayne.

Wayne heard Laura's scornful sniff. Then the professor said, "We have no further business to transact with you, sir."

"Heh, could be that's right," Girt agreed. "I reckon my business is with Saddler here."

"You got no business with me either," Wayne said coldly.

Beneath the brim of his Plainsman, Girt's leathery face was stubbled with rough fur. Sometime trapper, bounty hunter, and gunslick, Girt had a mean reputation in the Territory. Up this close, Wayne could smell the rank, unwashed scent of him.

"Oh, I got business with you, all right, Saddler," he persisted. "You see, I was all set to escort these fine folks around Poteau Mountain, until that stinking lawdog Thomas butted in. Now I don't cotton to you slinking in on his coattails and stealing my clients."

"Clients?" Wayne echoed dryly. "You're giving yourself airs, Girt."

Girt's lips went even thinner. "Don't go using your fancy talk on me, Saddler," he hissed. "I ain't going to take it. Just like I ain't going to take you sneaking behind my back so as to have these folks hire you."

Wayne bit back a sigh. Girt was on the prod, sure enough, and jawing with him wasn't going to be enough to satisfy him. Whether it was legitimate anger over losing a job as a guide, or whether the ominous handful of hard cases watching from in front of the saloon had anything to do with it, Wayne didn't know. But he reckoned he was about out of choices now.

"You'll take it, all right, Girt," he said tightly. "And you'll lap it up like a cat going after cream."

"Why, you stinking, lowdown clod stomper!" Girt snarled. "I'll take your blood, is what I'll take!"

He lunged at Wayne's throat, leading with a slamming right fist, exactly as a big cat might swipe with its paw to batter aside defenses and

25

open a target for its fangs.

Wayne slipped his head aside from the swing and felt it maul past his ear. But the driving lunge of Girt's hard body drove him back against the board wall of the general store. He heard Laura Hastings cry out, then Girt's hands clamped on his neck in a wicked hold — thumbs at his throat, fingers digging behind his ear — that bid fair to cut off both air and blood in a matter of seconds. Girt's stubbled face leered fiercely at him. If the guide's first blow had landed solidly the fight might be all but over. It still might, Wayne thought desperately.

Wayne set his shoulders against the wall, ignored the awful pressure on his throat, and hooked his fists, right and left, into Girt's leathery gut. The expression on Girt's vicious face changed to a grimace of pain and shock.

Wayne lifted his right fist between the bowed arms in an uppercut that packed all his shoulder behind it. Girt's head snapped back. His grip weakened. Instantly Wayne shot both arms up overhead and hammered his fists down on Girt's arms, pounding them down and away so the cruel fingers were torn free from his neck.

Girt cursed, bent low, snatched at one of Wayne's legs, and tried to pull it from under him. Wayne braced his legs and again hammered down, this time both fists — left wrapped around his right — at the base of Girt's neck. Girt's tattered Plainsman fell off. Wayne gripped his shoulders to hold him steady and brought his knee surging up into Girt's face, shoving outward with both arms as he did so.

Girt was snapped erect and reeled back a couple of steps. Wayne circled clear of the wall. Girt fought like a wrestler, and Wayne didn't fancy being hemmed up by him again.

His long, tangled hair swinging free now, Girt stalked him in a crouch, half-open hands out in front of him. Suddenly he sprang again. He slashed a left fist around at Wayne's side as his right hand clawed at Wayne's face and eyes. Wayne wheeled clear of the attack and dug his own right into Girt's buckskins just below his ribs. Girt grunted, twisted like a snake striking again at prey that had evaded it, and grabbed, low and dirty, with both hands.

Wayne pivoted aside. Girt's lunge carried him past, and Wayne snagged his bony right wrist in his own right hand as the guide went by. Immediately he jammed his left fist against Girt's shoulder joint, using the leverage to crank Girt's captured arm up behind his back. Catching Girt's other shoulder before he could twist free, Wayne ran him forward in the direction of his lunge, levering up on his captured arm to bend him forward as he did so. Headfirst, he ran Girt smack into the wall of the general store. A small cloud of dust rose from the old boards at the impact. Girt sagged in Wayne's grip.

He knew a few wrestling tricks of his own, Wayne mused with grim satisfaction.

He didn't cotton to hitting a man who was already whipped, so he backed off a pace, then another.

It was a mistake. Girt shook his head, mouthing low, bitter curses. Then he shoved against the ground and swiveled up onto his feet, his hand darting to his waist as he rose. When he came fully around to face Wayne, the naked ten-inch blade of his bowie knife gleamed in his fist.

Wayne's reaction was automatic. The years hadn't dulled his reflexes as a fighting man. His own bowie was in his hand and extended in the old fighting stance before he even realized it fully. The brass strip laid along the back of the blade, just behind the false edge, caught the sunlight and flashed like gold.

Girt sneered as he saw it. "Got your sticker all prettied up," he jeered. "Won't help you none, though."

"Won't it?" Wayne said coolly.

Girt moved like he knew how to use his big blade. Wayne had heard stories about his skill with it, and the stories looked to be true. Girt didn't seem even a little flustered at facing a man who moved just like he did. Maybe he had even been expecting it.

"Come on, Saddler, let's see how good you are with that fancy blade!" Girt snarled. He made little circling motions with the tip of his bowie.

"Let's see how your knife stacks up against this sawed-off," a new voice cut in harshly. "Back away, Girt, or I'll cut you in two!"

Girt had to risk a glance at this new threat.

Wayne followed the flick of his eyes. Deputy U.S. Marshal Heck Thomas had appeared like a conjurer's trick in a carnival sideshow and stood just at the corner of the general store. The double-barreled shotgun he gripped in both hands was steady as a rock. Its twin barrels were lined square on Girt Tannery.

Slowly Girt straightened out of his knife fighter's crouch, his mouth working angrily. He didn't like it, but even he wasn't going to buck a dead drop by a sawed-off handled by the likes of Heck Thomas.

"Sheath the knife and get out of here," Heck commanded. "A little brawling's one thing. Knife fighting on the main street is something else again. You're lucky I'm still letting you run around loose. Next time I just might let Wayne here have you."

Girt cursed under his breath but complied. Wayne cut a look toward the saloon. The audience in front of it had disappeared, including the figure in the duster. He sheathed his own blade as Girt snatched up his hat and limped in that direction.

Wayne turned as Laura ran up to him.

"Are you all right?" she gasped, worry already starting to give way to relief.

"No harm done." Wayne remembered Girt's cruel hands at his neck. Things had been closer than he wanted to admit.

"You acquitted yourself admirably," Hastings praised as he stepped forward with a bit more reserve than his daughter.

"Yeah," Heck's voice drawled. "You looked almost as good as you did back in the old days." The lawman had advanced a little from his position at the corner of the building. The sawed-off sagged casually under his arm.

"Thanks for the assist," Wayne told him. He frowned. "I figured you'd be headed back to Poteau by now."

"I rode over here with the professor and his daughter," Heck explained. "When I saw Girt and those other yahoos hanging around, I reckoned I might better do the same."

"Is Girt riding with those fellows at the saloon?"

"You spotted them, huh?"

"I spotted them."

"Maybe you *are* still just as good as you used to be." Heck grinned.

Wayne glanced again at the saloon. He hoped he wasn't going to have a chance to find out if Heck was right.

CHAPTER 3

"Girt's been keeping bad company of late," Heck told Wayne, settling his shoulders against the straight back of his chair and stretching his long legs out under the café table where they sat. "He's been running with a pack of owlhoots headed up by Nolen Driver. That was them over to the saloon."

Wayne sipped at his coffee. Its fragrant aroma helped to clear the stench of Girt Tannery from his nostrils. From their seats in the café he could keep an eye on the saloon through the dusty window. So far, neither Girt nor any of the other hard cases had shown themselves again, for which Wayne was grateful.

He and Heck Thomas had left Hastings and his daughter to the job of selecting the supplies at the store. At Heck's suggestion, the two men had headed over to the café for coffee.

"I've heard of Driver," Wayne said. "But he's new to these parts, isn't he?"

Heck nodded. "He and his bunch have been operating up in the northeast part of the Territory, mostly spreading wide loops and hitting an occasional bank in some isolated town. There's nothing we can prove; he's too careful for that.

But we know it's him just the same. I'm not too happy at having him turn up here. Could be things were getting too hot for him up north." Heck lifted his cup reflectively. "He's a bad one, sure enough. Word is, he packs a sword that he likes to use on folks who get crossways of him."

"Must be that cavalry saber I spotted on one of the horses when I rode in."

"Likely," Heck agreed. "He brags about having been in the cavalry. Has his men call him Captain." Heck snorted. "Truth is, he never made officer rank at all. He did manage a dishonorable discharge for getting drunk and sticking that sword through an unarmed reservation Indian one night."

"You think Driver and Girt are in cahoots?"

Heck frowned. "Hard to say. Girt's always been pretty much of a lone wolf. But it would be worthwhile to keep an eye out for Driver and his cronies, even though I can't see why they'd have any interest in Hastings and his Viking artifacts."

"They might have an interest in his daughter," Wayne suggested darkly.

Heck shook his head. "Driver's bad, but he takes that officer business pretty seriously. I've never heard of him allowing a woman to be mistreated."

"I hope you're right," Wayne said.

Heck drained the last of his coffee. "Guess I'll mosey on," he said as he rose. "The professor and his daughter are in good hands now, and there's big trouble with Bill Doolin and his gang back near Guthrie. I hear the marshal's planning to sic me, Bill Tilghman, and Chris

Madsen on their tail."

"The Oklahoma Guardsmen," Wayne drawled, repeating the nickname given to the legendary trio of lawmen. "Bill Doolin better watch his step."

Heck winced. "It's a mighty sorry thing when three hardworking peace officers are stuck with a moniker like that. Be seeing you, Wayne. Keep a cartridge under the hammer."

"I always do."

The aging lawman moved to the door and checked both ways before stepping out on the street. Moments later he jogged past on his big gray, headed out of town.

Wayne watched him go as he brooded over what Heck had told him. He wasn't looking to cross paths with Driver. Like Heck had said, there didn't seem much chance of the outlaw taking any interest in his charges. But having the man in the area at all made him uneasy.

A movement down the street caught Wayne's eye. He sat up a little straighter as he saw a trio of men emerge from the saloon. The leader looked to be the hombre in the white duster. He led the way as they angled in the direction of the café.

A clatter of dishes at a nearby table brought Wayne's head around. The small, balding proprietor of the café had also seen the oncoming men. His hands shook a little as he cleared the table, and he looked anxiously in Wayne's direction. The only other patrons in the café were a pair of old-timers at a corner table. They, too, seemed to have noted the approach of the trio.

As they drew nearer, Wayne had a chance to study them through the smudged glass. Their leader was a tall, handsome man with broad shoulders, lean waist, long legs, and erect bearing. A full mustache adorned his face. Black hair showed beneath the brim of the cavalry hat he wore, and Wayne glimpsed regulation cavalry boots and pants beneath the flapping tails of the duster. He had the sudden impression that the thin coat was worn habitually to protect the military garb from dust and dirt.

His two cronies were gun-toting hard cases of the type Wayne had dealt with more often than he cared to remember in his days as a lawman. Grim-eyed and mean, such yahoos were usually a good hand with six-shooters and fists, and not given to worrying much about fair play in using them. They'd bear watching in any sort of fracas.

Wayne shifted in his chair and let his right hand dangle at his side.

The leader entered the café, bracketed by his followers. The interior of the establishment suddenly seemed smaller. The trio paused just inside the door and surveyed the room with the searching gazes of men who lived by the cock of the hammer and the pull of the trigger.

Up this close, Wayne could see the signs of age and wear on the cavalry gear. The once sky-blue pants were faded and threadbare. A holstered revolver rode easily on a wide black belt.

The leader motioned his cronies toward a separate table, then strode in Wayne's direction. A tight smile showed beneath his mustache. "Wayne Saddler?" he greeted. "I'm Nolen Driver."

Wayne used a booted foot to shove a chair out from the far side of the table. "Have a seat."

Driver hadn't offered to shake hands. Wayne didn't either. He kept his right hanging free by his side as Driver accepted his invitation. The two hard cases had occupied the other table. One of them held an eye on the door and the windows. The other squinted about the room. Driver had some good hands backing him.

"Smoke?" Driver produced a slender cheroot. He fired it up with a lucifer when Wayne shook his head to decline. The acrid smoke touched Wayne's nostrils.

"I saw you tangle with Girt." Driver blew more smoke. "You handled him pretty good."

"He running with you?" Wayne asked.

"Girt's a hothead. I wouldn't want him riding under my command on a permanent basis. But, for right now, I'm hoping he can help me out."

"How might that be?"

Driver leaned back and studied Wayne appraisingly over the smoldering cheroot. "I want to get your opinion on that very thing," he said then.

What was Driver aiming at? Wayne wondered. "I'm listening."

"I'm new to these parts. Girt came to me with a tale, and I'm wondering if it's on the up and up."

"What tale?"

"He says there's gold on Poteau Mountain.

Enough gold so as to make it worthwhile to put some effort into getting it out. But he claims he can't do it alone for fear of owlhoots learning about what he's doing and moving in on him. Says the mountain is full of jaspers who'd kill a man without a second thought for a gold strike. He came to me for protection. We split whatever we take out."

Wayne shook his head skeptically. "From what I've heard of you, Driver, I never figured you'd be taking up prospecting."

Driver chuckled. "I guess you must've picked up some of the talk from up north." He plucked the thin cigar from his mouth and jabbed it forward for emphasis. "It's amazing what folks will say about a man who won't let himself be roped and tied like every other horse in the herd."

"You're just a wild bronc, huh?" Wayne said dryly.

Driver didn't get his back up. "Now, don't get me wrong," he cautioned. "I'm no greenhorn. I've seen the elephant, and been back to see it again, but I'm not the owlhoot Heck Thomas and some of the rest of the lawdogs would like to make me out to be. Sure, I've ridden the edge of the law; lots of men in these parts have — probably you, too. That doesn't make me an outlaw. No, it just seems Thomas and his ilk have bitten off more than they can chew in trying to tame this territory. It's a lot easier to blame all the holdups and bank robberies and rustled stock on a few free-living men like me and Bill Doolin than it is to admit to the governor that there's more outlaws and desperadoes in this region than they could corral in a month of Sundays." His lip curled almost mockingly.

"And you're not one of them," Wayne concluded.

Driver's eyes narrowed briefly. "Like you said, just a wild bronc running free." He grinned his tight grin. "But even rumors and old wives' tales can mean trouble when they get the lawdogs sniffing around your backtrail. That's why I came to these parts — thought maybe I could clean some of the old dirt off my boots and start fresh."

"Best of luck," Wayne said.

Driver pulled on his cheroot. "I make my own luck. Like this business with Girt. Before I get in the traces with him, I want your opinion."

Wayne eyed him. "Why me?"

Driver leaned forward a little in his chair. His dark eyes were intent. "I've heard tell of you since I've been in these parts. They say you're ex-cavalry. That speaks high of a man, and it makes us brothers. I've served under the crossed sabers myself, you know." Pride rode his voice.

"So I heard." Wayne didn't push for details. He didn't want to think of himself as a brother to this man.

Something that looked like disappointment flickered in Driver's expression. He eased back in his chair a bit, but tension was still evident in the lean lines of his figure. "I also hear you know this land as well as anybody — even the Indians who used to live here. What about it? Is Girt giving me the straight stuff? Is there really gold on Poteau Mountain?" The cheroot in his mouth bobbed as he chawed down hard on it.

"There was a mine up there a few years back," Wayne told him. "But it petered out after a spell. I guess what Girt's telling you could be the truth."

Driver settled back, nodding thoughtfully. "Good enough. I'm still not sure I'd trust Girt to stand guard duty, but I don't reckon it would hurt to take a look at whatever he wants to show us." Driver cocked his head. "Wouldn't hurt to have another man along to keep an eye on Girt, either; that is, another man who knows that mountain. What do you say, Saddler? You willing to sign on under my command? I'd pay top fighting-man wages for your services, maybe even let you in on a cut of any gold we find."

Wayne held back a frown. "I've already been hired," he said, watching Driver carefully.

Driver chuckled easily. "Sure. Girt told me that Eastern professor and his pretty daughter were paying you to take them up the mountain looking for some sort of geegaws. Viking artifacts, isn't it?"

"Yep."

"You think there's anything to all that business about Vikings?" Driver asked skeptically. "Sounds pretty far-fetched to me."

Driver seemed mighty interested in his new employment, Wayne reflected. "There's some old inscriptions up there the professor claims might've been made by Vikings," he temporized.

"Is that what they call Indian Rock?"

"Yeah, that's it."

Driver drew thoughtfully at his cheroot. "I guess no one really knows what you might find up on that peak." Then he grinned. "Maybe Girt will even lead me and my command to some gold." He rose to his feet with a swish of his duster and sketched a quick salute. The disappointed look touched his face again when Wayne didn't respond. "So long, Saddler. Could be our trails will cross up there."

"Could be," Wayne allowed.

Driver strode toward the door. "Jake, Ben, move out," he ordered in passing.

The two hard cases cast wary looks once more in Wayne's direction, then rose and followed in their commander's wake. Scowling, Wayne watched Driver lead them back to the saloon, where they disappeared into the bar.

Wayne looked up and shook his head as the café proprietor approached with a steaming pot of coffee.

"They're bad ones," the proprietor offered with a nervous grin. "They like to tore up the saloon the other night."

Down the street, Driver and a half dozen followers emerged from the bar and swung onto their waiting horses. Wayne spotted Girt Tannery's faded buckskins. He watched as they rode out of town. A cloud of dust hung in their trail.

"Good riddance, I say," the proprietor commented with feeling.

Wayne got up, left a coin on the table, nodded at the man's thanks, and stepped back out on the street. Hastings and his daughter were just coming out of the store with their arms full of bundles. A teenage boy was lugging out more behind them. Wayne crossed to give them a hand as they began to pack the supplies on the mule.

Laura checked items off the supply list as Hastings passed them to Wayne to be loaded. The professor hefted the bundles almost as easily as the stock boy had done. A spark gleamed in his eye and he grinned at Wayne as they worked.

"I'll go settle up with the storekeeper," he said as Wayne tightened the rope over the last bundle. He entered the store with a spring in his step.

Wayne turned to check the ropes one more time. The mule cocked a cynical eye back at him.

"All done?" Laura asked.

Wayne looked about to find Laura watching him. She smiled as she caught his gaze. "Dad's eager to get started," she said. "So am I."

Wayne noted the pistol in a shiny new holster at her slender waist. "What did you pick out?" He nodded at the sidearm.

"A thirty-two, like you suggested." She palmed the weapon with the easy caution of an old hand with firearms. Butt first, she extended it to him.

Wayne examined the gun and recognized it as one of the recently issued Colt New Pocket Double Action Revolvers. He was a little surprised that the general store had it in stock. Nodding his approval, he returned it to Laura.

She slipped it back into her holster, then reached to touch Wayne's forearm. "I saw those men go into the café," she said with evident concern. "What did they want?"

Wayne gazed in the direction where Driver and his pack had vanished. "I wish I knew," he answered bleakly.

CHAPTER 4

"Poteau," Hastings remarked as he glanced up at the wooded slope towering above them. "That's a French word. It translates as stake or post. It could also be used for a place of execution. Curious."

Wayne nodded and urged his paint a little ahead to lead the ascent. Hastings and his daughter put their horses in behind him.

"French trappers named it when they first came to this area," Wayne explained over his shoulder. "The whole region belonged to the Choctaw before it was opened for settlement. I reckon there have been tales about folks disappearing, secret outlaw hideouts, and lost caves on the mountain ever since those days."

"Do you put any credence in such stories?"

Wayne hitched his shoulders. "Who knows? Don't guess anybody can tell for sure if any of the stories are true or not."

The peak was only one of several small mountains and large hills that thrust up incongruously from the grasslands. They were scattered like huge humps over an area of dozens of square miles. The very strangeness of the formations gave them an air of mystery.

At that moment his nape prickled. He glanced warily about the forest of blackjack oaks, elms, and occasional evergreens. A flutter of movement became the dancing white tail of a deer's retreating hindquarters. But before he could point it out, the animal had bounded away among the trees. He shook his head. He was getting a mite jumpy when a deer could spook him, he thought wryly.

"What did you see?" Laura asked from behind him.

Her perception impressed him. "A deer." He pointed with his chin. "Gone now."

"Oh, I'm sorry I missed it."

"Most of these tales you mention are probably just folklore and superstition," Hastings said, getting back to the question about the stories. "The existence of caves doesn't seem likely, unless they were dug by men. This mountain appears to be mostly sandstone and would not lend itself naturally to the formation of caves."

"Never seen one of them myself," Wayne said noncommittally.

With a clatter of hooves, Laura urged her palomino up beside him. Her leg brushed his briefly before she shifted her mount clear, but she didn't seem to have noticed the contact. Her hat was pulled back off her head and held by a cord around her neck. Sunshine, peeking through the new leaves overhead, dappled her black hair with glinting highlights.

"You like this country, don't you?" she asked with evident interest.

43

She seemed to be able to read him like a skilled tracker could read signs, Wayne noted with amusement.

"Yeah," he answered. "A man gets a sense of freedom out here."

"And that's important to you?"

He nodded. "Being in the cavalry makes a man appreciate discipline and teamwork, but it also makes him appreciate being able to make his own decisions once he gets out."

"Deputy Thomas said you were stationed here in the Territory." She was watching him as she spoke, guiding her horse by feel with the skill of a good rider.

"I spent some time at Camp Supply when this was still Indian land." He was pleased by her interest; it was easy to keep talking to her. "Most of the Indian troubles had been settled by then, but we were still responsible for keeping the peace. I was an old hand at hunting down outlaws and desperadoes in these parts before I ever pinned on a deputy's badge."

He thought of the heavily laden pack mule plodding stolidly behind them. This present excursion was a luxury trip, compared to some of the patrols he had ridden on with other troopers. Their supplies and equipment had often been limited to not much more than a cavalry-issue blanket, a canteen, seven days' rations, a Spencer repeating rifle, a Colt Army revolver, and a stock of ammunition for both. He recalled a line from an old cavalry ballad. How had it gone? "Forty miles a day on beans and hay." That sure fit the life of a cavalryman, all right.

Laura looked to be on the verge of asking something further, but her father's voice cut in again. "How far is it to the rune stone?"

Laura let her horse drop back a little.

"About halfway up the mountain," Wayne answered.

"Very well."

The meager trail they had been following grew steeper. Wayne held his weight up off the saddle to make it easier going for the paint. He could feel the smooth roll and play of the animal's muscles beneath his legs. Of Indian pony stock, the horse moved with the surefootedness of a mountain cat.

At a level spot he reined up and twisted in the saddle to look back down the mountain. He could make out the brownish blur of Heavener in the distance. He let his eyes roam over their backtrail as Laura and her father drew even with him.

"Another deer?" Laura turned to follow the direction of his gaze.

"Just getting the lay of the land," he replied. It had been in Wayne's mind that Girt Tannery, smarting from the licking he had taken, might have gotten a notion to dog their tracks, looking for a chance to even the score. He didn't mention the possibility aloud.

Laura grew solemn, as though she had suddenly grasped the purpose of his halt.

He felt the shrewd eyes of her and her father

on him. Their backtrail looked clear. Wordlessly he heeled the paint around.

"What would've brought Vikings this far inland, Professor?" he asked as they resumed the climb.

"They were inveterate explorers," Hastings said. He sounded pleased to have a chance to address the topic. "Their ancestors were seafarers as far back as three thousand B.C. Icelandic sagas record them reaching Canada around one thousand A.D. Actually, they were probably there much earlier. It requires no great leap of theorizing to believe they also reached the eastern coast of what is now the United States."

"That's a long way from Poteau Mountain," Wayne pointed out.

"Not when you consider they crossed an entire ocean to reach these shores. From the coast, driven by their relentless urge to explore and find booty, an intrepid band of them could easily have sailed their ships up the Mississippi River, and then on up the Arkansas and its tributaries to bring them into this region. Indeed, there is nothing to have prevented them from traveling overland to reach this point."

Nothing except a thousand miles of foreign, hostile wilderness, Wayne mused. But, by all accounts, the Vikings had been a hardy folk, and the prospect of new realms to pillage might easily have lured them on.

"Do you think you can decipher the stone?" he asked aloud.

A couple of seconds slipped by before Hastings

answered. "I must see it first," he said then. "I've made a study of runic translations, and I've seen a sketch of the characters on the stone. I'm not certain it was accurate, but if it was, there are elements that puzzle me."

He didn't offer any more explanation, and Wayne let it drop because once again his neck tingled with a feral sense of unease. He ran his gaze over the wooded terrain. No deer this time, but he had ridden the manhunter's trail too long to ignore the sensation.

"Keep climbing," he ordered without preamble, and turned the paint aside into the woods.

He heard Laura's half-uttered query, but the sound of their horses' hooves continued. Not looking back, he sent the paint angling up the steeper slope through the timber. He shifted his reins to his left hand and let his right stay near the butt of his Colt. There wasn't a lot of underbrush, but there was still plenty of cover among the trees, enough so that a rifle wouldn't be of much use.

But there had to be a target for a gun to be of any use at all. His probing eyes found no betraying movement; his straining ears caught only the rustle of a breeze and the sound of his own horse. He pulled to a halt and studied the thin carpet of dead leaves on the ground. There was no trace of the passage of man or animal.

The sensation of being hunted finally faded. Wayne frowned. He doubted Girt Tannery could have eluded him so completely, but he was certain he hadn't imagined the presence of a stalker. But whoever or whatever it was had slipped away like a ghost.

Maybe some of the dark tales about the mountain were true.

At last he swung the paint about and headed back to the trail. His charges had obeyed his orders; they were still working their way up the slope. Both of them turned questioning looks his way as he rejoined them.

"Just checking," he offered shortly, then resumed his place at the head of their little column. He still rode left-handed.

Another quarter mile up the mountain he took them off the trail and in among the trees.

"Canyon's this way," he said tersely.

"Just a minute, if you please," Hastings requested.

Wayne drew up. The professor nudged his horse near a lichen-covered outcropping of gray-black stone that bulged from the ground to almost the height of a mounted man. Leaning from his saddle, he peered closely at the massive boulders.

Wayne glanced at Laura. She was intent on her father. Her head was tilted slightly, and there was an air of expectancy about her.

Hastings murmured something to himself and dismounted without taking his eyes off the rocks.

"Laura, my brush," he demanded in clipped tones.

Obediently she slid from her mare and went quickly to the pack mule. In a moment she had produced a stiff-bristled brush, something like what might be used to groom a horse. Hastings had approached the rocks and was leaning a little forward as he continued his inspection. Hearing his daughter's approach, he reached backward with an open hand, and she placed the brush in it.

Hastings took the utensil and applied its stiff bristles gently to the face of the rock, working it back and forth with sure, easy strokes. Particles of moss and lichen drifted to the ground at his feet.

Wayne bent forward in his saddle to watch: The pair's preoccupation was contagious. Plainly, they had worked like this many times before.

Wayne pulled his eyes away and surveyed the slope above them. He saw nothing of consequence, and no warning tingle touched his neck. He edged the paint closer as Hastings shifted the brush to his left hand and ran his fingers over the scoured face of the stone.

"Can you seem them?" he demanded urgently of his daughter.

She squinted. "I'm not sure, Dad," she said hesitantly.

"Here, feel." He caught her wrist and guided her hand over the same area he had touched. "Well?"

She shook her head. "I just can't tell. Maybe there's something there, maybe not."

Hastings trailed his fingers fleetingly over the stone again. For just a heartbeat Wayne fancied his own eyes detected the traces of straight, geometric lines forming squarish figures carved into the stone. Then the impression vanished.

"I'm almost certain," Hastings declared. He shook his head ruefully and his shoulders sagged. He looked up at the branches that diffused the sunlight. "Perhaps if the light were better, I could tell for sure." Cocking his head at Wayne, he asked, "How much farther, Mr. Saddler?"

"Just up there a ways," Wayne told him. Gazing at the outcropping now he could no longer discern the strange figures. "You think there might've been some runes carved there?" he asked, nodding at the bare patch of rock.

"I thought I detected traces under the lichen," Hastings confirmed. "I'm used to looking for such things, and frequently where you find runes carved in one spot, you will find others in the same vicinity."

"Any carving on those rocks was done a mighty long time ago," Wayne commented.

"Centuries ago," Hastings agreed. "Ample time for erosion and wind and rain to have erased them on this slope where they are exposed to the elements."

Wayne felt a spectral touch similar to his earlier sensation of being watched. How many years had this outcropping and its phantom markings awaited their coming? And how had Hastings managed to spot them, if they existed at all, under the lichens and moss?

"Come on, Dad," Laura urged. "I'll return and clean the rock properly so you can examine it later." She was clearly eager to get his mind off his disappointment. "We're almost to the big rune stone. Let's go see it."

Hastings nodded crisply. "Of course, you're right." He grinned briefly at Wayne. "Forgive a scientist's dedication to fieldwork."

"Take your time," Wayne said.

But Hastings was already swinging astride his mount. "Lead on, sir."

Wayne complied. Single file, they threaded their way through the timber until Wayne drew up and pointed. "There's the canyon mouth."

At some time in the distant past, long before the mysterious stone carvers had passed this way, a great rift had opened in the side of the mount, creating a secluded ravine that cut far back into the rock. The mouth of the canyon was choked with trees, and only a man with a trained eye or one who knew these parts could pick it out on the wooded mountainside. Even Wayne, relying on memories a couple years old, almost missed it.

Wordlessly he turned the paint in among the thicker growth. In moments great rocky walls seemed to grow silently out of the forest on either side of them, towering fifty feet above their heads. Wayne heard Laura's gasp of surprise as she became aware of their imposing height.

The walls gave fine cover for a bushwhacker, Wayne reflected, and it would be easy for an enemy to hem up anything or anybody in the canyon. He had the sudden feeling he was riding into a trap. Resolutely he put the notion aside.

Ahead through the trees, in the shelter of the canyon wall, he saw a dark looming shape.

"There." He leveled a finger. "That's Indian Rock."

CHAPTER 5

"Magnificent," Hastings said with a sigh.

He stepped back from his close scrutiny of the carven figures to take in the whole stone.

Seeing it again, Wayne was just as impressed as he had been when he had first come upon the stone. Given the professor's commitment to his calling, he could imagine what this initial sight of it must mean to the older man.

Standing upright like a gigantic signboard, Indian Rock towered twelve feet high by ten feet wide. In places it was almost a foot and a half thick. At a height of five feet — just right for a stone carver to stand and work — eight characters stretched almost six feet across the face of the stone. They were composed of angles, lines, and triangles. Reading from left to right, they increased in size from six inches to nine inches. Silent and enigmatic, the strange figures offered their mysterious message as they had for centuries.

"The rock itself must've fallen from up there eons ago and landed upright in this position." Hastings tipped back his pith helmet and tilted his head to stare up at the cliff behind the stone.

"The canyon walls and its vertical position would've served to protect it from weathering,"

Laura added. She looked almost as awestruck as her father.

"Yet there are still signs of aging." Hastings drew closer to the stone and traced one of the characters almost reverently with a fingertip. "Note how smooth and round the edges are. Given the protected conditions in the canyon, these characters may even predate those on the rocks outside." He turned to Wayne. "This is an extraordinary find. Thank you for consenting to bring us here."

Wayne shifted his weight uncomfortably. "What do you think?" He nodded at the characters. "Can you make any sense of them?"

Lines furrowed the professor's brow. He contemplated the huge stone and its writings a moment before replying. "The sketches I saw were accurate, but I must study this further. There is something here that does not make sense." He fell silent, lost in speculation.

"I'll get to setting up camp," Wayne said.

"Let me help you," Laura offered quickly.

Wayne used his head to indicate her father. "Won't he be needing you?"

She smiled wryly. "Not at this point. Believe me, he'd appreciate being left alone with this find for a while."

Wayne grinned back at her. "Sounds like you know his ways well."

"He's taken me with him into the field ever since I was a little girl. Most of my schooling came from him. I grew up on college campuses and archaeological sites in this country and Europe." For an instant a shadow appeared to touch her dark eyes, then it disappeared in the glow of her smile. "Let's get busy."

Absorbed in his work, Hastings didn't seem to notice their departure. Laura pitched to the task of unloading the mule and setting up camp with a good spirit. A clearing under the trees within view of the stone made a natural campsite.

"You've done this before," Wayne surmised as she held the final stake for the second of the two tents. She hadn't flinched once as he'd used the hammer to pound the stakes home.

She looked up at him from where she knelt. Her smile made him catch his breath before he swung the hammer again.

"Many times," she assured him. "Heavens, this is luxury compared to some of the accommodations I've had on archaeological digs."

Wayne landed a final stroke, then clamped a fist about the stake. It held firm under his grip.

"That's set," he announced.

Laura rose smoothly to her feet at almost the same moment as he straightened, and for a single breath they were very close. She stepped back with an uncertain smile.

"I'll see to putting up the supplies," she said as she turned away trimly. She hesitated, glancing back over her shoulder. "Which tent is mine? There'll be room in it for storage."

Wayne gestured. "Take your pick."

"This one looks nice." She ducked into it. In

a moment her head reappeared. "I'll be happy here."

"A spring for fresh water is yonder under that ledge," Wayne said.

He watched her trot over to the supplies and begin to sort them. Glancing in the direction of the rune stone, he saw Hastings just turning back to his examination, as though he had taken a moment to observe their work in setting up the camp.

Things looked to be in good hands here, Wayne decided. He crossed to where he had hobbled the horses. The paint looked at him disapprovingly as he tightened the cinch.

"Had enough of us already?" Laura's light tone carried genuine curiosity.

Wayne came about to find her watching him from where she sorted the supplies. "Thought I'd scout around outside the ravine for a spell," he explained as he finished adjusting the cinch.

"Looking for outlaws and desperadoes?"

"You never know." He put a foot in the stirrup and mounted, then nudged his horse closer to her. "Stay here in the canyon, and keep an eye peeled for strangers. Don't put your gun out of reach. If you have trouble, fire off a round. I'll be within earshot. Tell your dad I'll be back shortly."

She grew more serious. "Do you really think there's any danger for us here?"

Wayne hitched his shoulders. "Not likely to have any trouble. This canyon's pretty secluded unless you know it's here. We should be safe enough so long as we don't get careless."

Laura's expression was sober. "I'll keep an eye on things."

Wayne didn't doubt it. He wheeled the paint.

"Be careful," Laura called softly.

He lifted a hand in parting, then headed out the way they had come. There was no other route out of the ravine. The walls made a neat three-sided box.

Once clear of the walls, he angled upslope to cut the trail they had followed up the mountain. The face of Poteau Mountain was pocked with many small rifts and ravines. Wayne doubted whether any man knew them all. It was one of the things that made the mount an ideal sanctuary for hombres on the dodge from the law.

Above the canyon, he left the trail and began to ride systematically back and forth across the slope, dividing his attention between the surrounding terrain and the ground underfoot.

Sheer scars left by ancient landslides and steep grades created by erosion forced frequent detours. At times, the paint's hooves slipped on bare rock and loose stone, threatening to plunge them both in the wake of the landslides.

Squirrels and birds frolicked among the branches of the trees, and once he startled another deer. He spotted traces of other animal life, from the distinctive pug mark of a cougar to the churned soil and leaves left by a pack of razorback hogs. He ignored such signs. He was looking for other prey.

At last he spotted the telltale traces he sought,

and his mouth tightened. Within the last few days, a mounted man had ridden lazily along here, headed toward the summit. Hoofprints were clearly visible in the shallow layer of soft soil and the disturbed leaves. Wayne turned the paint along the stranger's trail.

It was easy to follow, and he rode more carefully, pausing at intervals to listen and watch, and to sniff the breeze blowing down from the heights. When his nostrils flared with a familiar stench, he reined up. Carried on the wind were the mingled odors of horseflesh, spoiled food, and human waste, sure signs of a poorly kept camp.

Gently he heeled the paint into the breeze. Another seventy-five yards and he saw where the ground dropped sharply away at the edge of some sort of crevice or defile. Even as he saw it, the first murmur of voices reached him.

Dismounting, he hitched the reins to a nearby tree and used an old kerchief to tie the paint's muzzle so it couldn't whinny. Then crouching, rifle in hand, he eased closer to the edge of the defile. Five yards back from the lip, he went to his belly, plucked off his Stetson, and snaked the rest of the way forward.

At the edge of the drop-off he could peer down into a draw some forty feet deep. Beneath an overhang of rock on the far wall were a dead fire and a clutter of gear. A trio of hobbled horses grazed farther up the draw.

The owners of the horses were lounging lethargically about their camp. They were a sorry-looking outfit, Wayne thought. All three of them wore shabby, soiled range gear and showed several days' growth of whiskers. To a man, they packed side-arms, and one of them, a burly jasper seated on a boulder, was using what looked like a Mexican-style machete to chop at the ground with bored disinterest.

"I've about got my gutful of all this," the man was saying. "We been cooling our heels up here for nigh onto two weeks. When in tarnation do you figure the heat'll be off from that bank job?"

"Relax, Zeb." Straining, Wayne caught the response of one of the others, a lean mustached hombre with two low-slung pistols. He was sprawled on his back with his head on a saddle and a hat over his eyes. "Won't be much longer now, I reckon, before it'll be safe to mosey down off this mountain." He sat up, then rose smoothly to his feet.

"Can't be too soon for me," Zeb grumbled. He raised his voice. "Pete, when you rode into town the other day, did anybody pay any mind to you? You see any lawdogs hanging around?"

"I already done told you, no," that worthy replied from his position in the shade of the ledge. He swigged from a bottle. "Shoot, folks down there ain't interested in a no-account bank holdup two weeks old and twenty miles away." He didn't sound very happy about the set of matters either.

Zeb's machete rose and fell methodically. Wayne could see large patches of rust on the blade.

"You boys are just chompin' at the bit to start

spending that money." The two-gun honcho swaggered closer, thumbs hooked in his gunbelt.

"That's the sure truth of it," Zeb asserted.

"Well, you just keep in mind that if I hadn't planned the job, neither of you would have any of that loot. Best we sit it out a few more days before we move on. That is, unless you got any better ideas, Zeb." His swagger had brought him near the seated Zeb, and he stood with legs spread, just out of range of the rusty blade.

"Naw, Shooter, I ain't got any better ideas," Zeb said uneasily. "I know you're the boss man of this outfit. I ain't looking to buck you."

Cocky in his authority, Shooter strutted down the draw a little ways. He pulled one of his pistols and twirled it deftly back into its holster. Then he began a series of quick draws, first one hand, then the other, then both at once. The guns flashed in the sunlight. He wasn't bad, Wayne allowed.

Zeb hefted his machete and eyed Shooter for a moment, then chopped the blade into the ground one more time before twisting his head about to address his other partner. "You got any more of that rotgut you picked up in town?"

"Couple of bottles," Pete told him.

Muttering, Zeb left his machete sticking upright in the dirt and lumbered under the overhang, where he produced a bottle from a tattered gunnysack.

Wayne had seen enough. He worked his way back from the edge of the draw. Rising, he clamped his Stetson on his head and started toward his paint. He frowned thoughtfully as he remounted.

The two-gun Shooter and his cronies were a den of snakes, right enough, and they'd bear watching. On the lam from their latest two-bit job, they would be dangerous if it came to a fracas. But none of them impressed him as being of the breed who could elude him as easily as the stalker had done. Unless his hunter's senses had betrayed him, there was still someone else lurking about this part of the mountain.

Brooding, Wayne took another swing farther up the grade, staying well clear of the outlaws' hideout. Once he got back down off the mountain, he'd have to let Heck or one of the other deputy marshals know about Shooter and his boys. But by then, they'd probably be long gone, especially if the restless Zeb had his druthers.

He wasn't sure when he first became aware of it this time. The sensation crept over him gradually, as if whoever was out there was being mighty careful not to watch him for too long at a time.

Wayne didn't let on. He kept riding, kept searching his surroundings and scanning the ground as he had been. All the while the unseen eyes were making his neck itch like fleas were crawling on it.

The stalker was behind him, he calculated, else he would have spotted him by now. He ground his teeth together. If the watcher wanted him dead, most likely he'd have a bullet in his skull by this time. The notion of being at someone's mercy galled him.

He gave no warning of what he planned, only laid the reins hard against the horse's neck and swiveled his body tight in the saddle. Well trained, light on its feet, the paint spun like a cat. Fifty yards distant, Wayne's squint caught just a glimpse of movement among the trees. He put heels to the paint and took off like he was leading a cavalry charge.

Expertly he sent the horse weaving among the trees, blood pounding in his veins at the success of his maneuver. Ahead, what might have been a human figure darted from tree to tree, then disappeared as though swallowed up by the earth.

Wayne pulled up hard as he saw that such a notion wasn't far wrong. Barely a yard in front of the paint's prancing hooves the ground dropped away, sheer and sharp, to a jumble of boulders and massive slabs of sandstone.

Wayne came off his horse in a combat dismount and went to one knee on the edge of the drop, rifle snugged to his shoulder.

Nothing moved in the tangle of stone below. The deep defile had been hidden by the steepness of the slope. The jungle of fallen rock and tilted stone ran to where it doglegged out of sight down the grade.

Wayne shook his head slowly. An agile man who knew the passes and crevices of that devil's playground could elude pursuit by a lone foe for as long as he took a hankering to. Wayne lowered his rifle in disgust. He doubted that he would have really fired on an unknown stranger doing his best to get away, but he still didn't have an inkling as to the fellow's motives for dogging his trail.

He rose to his feet. If he followed the rim of the draw he might yet catch another glimpse of the stalker, maybe even be able to run him to ground. But it was likely to take the rest of the day, if he succeeded at all, and he'd been away from the camp for a good spell.

He gazed up through the foliage at the sky. The sun was riding low. The phantom watcher would have to wait, he decided ruefully. With a scowl riding his features, he climbed back into the saddle and turned downhill toward the camp.

CHAPTER 6

"Where are you going?" Laura asked with what she hoped was a light tone. "Off on another patrol?"

Wayne glanced at her from over the saddle of his horse and grinned slightly. "That's right. All part of good military procedure."

His own tone was also light, but she fancied she read an underlying seriousness in the hard set of his features and the tautness of his broad shoulders.

She drew closer and asked, "Do you still believe we're in some sort of danger? This is the second day you've ridden out to scout the area. You told us about those three outlaws, but you said there's nothing to worry about so long as they don't know we're here." She heard a faint catch to her words. "Is there something you're not telling us?"

His face turned grave. "There's somebody out there keeping an eye on us," he said shortly. "I want to know who it is."

"Did you see him?"

"Only got a quick look. Not enough to tell much." His terseness betrayed the fact that he was displeased with what he undoubtedly viewed as his failure to do his job.

"Could it be that man Driver, or maybe even Girt?" she asked.

He shook his head firmly. "Girt's not that good," he said flatly, "and it's not the way Driver would operate."

"Have you seen any sign of Driver and his men?"

"Not a trace," he told her.

She was suddenly eager to get away from a subject that was unpleasant to him. "While you're gone, would it be all right if I went back to the rocks outside the canyon so I could examine them more closely?"

She sounded absurdly like a schoolgirl asking permission for an excursion, she reflected in the back of her mind. Strangely, the notion didn't upset her.

He frowned slightly. "It'd be best if neither of you left the camp without me. Wait till later. I'm just going to make a swing down the mountain a ways. I'll be back before noon. Then I'll go with you."

"All right." She was pleased by the prospect of an outing with him.

"Where's the professor?" he asked gruffly.

"He copied the characters and is working at deciphering them in the tent." She laughed with genuine fondness. "Heaven forbid that I should bother him while he's doing that!"

He grinned. "Hold down the fort," he advised, and swung lithely into the saddle. He sat his horse with a pleasing, natural skill.

She drew close enough to reach out and touch

his hand where it rested on the saddle horn. Her impulsive gesture embarrassed her so she stepped back.

She realized she was blushing as he disappeared among the trees. She admonished herself for flirting shamelessly with a man she had known only a few days, a man who had expressed no real romantic interest in her.

What would she do if he did? The question came unbidden. Part of her, she was forced to admit, would welcome such attentions. But another part faced the prospect with fear and trembling.

Her hectic upbringing had given her an excellent education in a number of fields, fluency in several languages, and accomplished formal social skills as the lady of the Hastings household. But she had virtually no experience at all with affairs of the heart. It was a lack that she regretted in her more pensive moments, and one that made her feel awkward and intimidated in Wayne's presence.

How nice it would have been to have met him in a more civilized setting, she reflected, where her social skills, etiquette, and the proprieties of society would have provided definite boundaries and guidelines for their relationship.

Resolutely she put these thoughts aside and set to tidying up the camp — one of her regular chores when she accompanied her father on a dig.

Finished, she found a flat rock for a table and turned her attention to a graphlike map of the canyon floor. She had already made precise measurements of the small ravine; now it remained to transpose them. When completed, the map could be used to mark the precise locations of any additional artifacts they discovered.

Recalling the outcropping where her father had detected other carvings, she realized she might well need to extend the scope of her topographical diagram beyond the canyon.

She glanced up from her work as the professor emerged from the tent he shared with Wayne. "How's the translation going, Dad?" she asked eagerly. Over the years she had caught at least a portion of his enthusiasm for his work.

Hastings massaged his temples with thumb and forefinger. "It's a most curious puzzle," he answered thoughtfully. "But it's one I feel I'm on the verge of solving. I thought a breath of fresh air might do me good." He looked about the camp as if dismissing the topic for the moment. "Where's Mr. Saddler?"

"He went to scout some more. This afternoon he's going to take me back to examine that outcropping you noticed outside the canyon."

Hastings didn't respond.

Laura cocked her head at him. "Why don't you call him Wayne?"

"He's merely a hired hand, Laura," Hastings said stiffly. "There's no need for such familiarity."

Before she could respond, he had turned and ducked his head to return to the tent.

Shrugging in bemusement, she let it go. Her father often became distracted and irritable when wrestling with some new archaeological conundrum, but in this instance his preoccupation had lingered for an unusually long time. She wondered what it was he found so puzzling about the runes. Despite his controversial theories, he was considered by his colleagues to be one of the leading authorities on runic translations.

He did not reappear to enlighten her, and she knew better than to disturb him. Humming an old hymn, she resumed her own work, pausing occasionally, in light of Wayne's repeated warnings, to look and listen for signs of danger.

Despite such concerns, she found herself enjoying the coolness of the shade under the trees, and the trills and warbles of the birds in their branches. Once she stopped her work to watch the acrobatics of two squirrels scampering about on the ground. They seemed oblivious to her presence until she laughed out loud at their antics. Then they scooted quickly up separate trunks to peer down at her and chatter in protest.

At last, with the morning edging past, she put aside her mapmaking to prepare a noon meal — another of her field chores.

"Coming into camp!" Wayne's voice called out from the mouth of the canyon.

"Just in time for lunch." She smiled as he appeared from among the trees. She felt a bit of awe at how silently he had been able to approach the camp on horseback.

"Looks mighty good." He grinned as he swung out of the saddle and admired the cornbread and beans she had prepared.

She was pleased at his praise, but there was a tautness to him that made her guess he had been unsuccessful in his quest. "Any luck?" she queried.

He shook his head and accepted the plate she offered. Settling down cross-legged with the plate in his lap, he tilted his hat back and sighed.

"Nary a sign of anything except deer and one old black bear," he reported. "If somebody is keeping an eye on us, I figure he must be coming from higher up the mountain to do it." He looked around as Hastings emerged from the tent. "Howdy, Professor."

"Mr. Saddler," Hastings returned the greeting.

He nodded formally in thanks as he took the plate Laura handed him. The two men spoke little during the meal. Laura caught herself surreptitiously comparing the two of them. Both were strong-willed, capable, and quite handsome. She studied Wayne the longest as she made this last observation.

Unexpectedly he raised his eyes as though feeling her gaze on him. Hastily she dropped her glance to her plate and prayed he wouldn't notice the blush she was sure was mounting her neck all the way to her ears.

"Best camp meal I've ever had," he declared.

Proper manners made her lift her head and smile politely. "Thank you." She was sure her blush hadn't abated one whit.

Hastings set his plate aside and rose. "I believe I'll take a break from translating and have a closer look hereabouts in the ravine," he announced.

"The map's almost finished, if you need to mark a site," Laura offered promptly.

"Very well." Without further discussion he strode off toward the rune stone.

"You ready to go take another look at that outcropping?" Wayne asked her.

"Let me clean up a little bit here."

Hurriedly she set to the task, gratified by Wayne's unsought assistance with his own plate. "You don't need to help," she objected.

"A man on the trail, or one who lives alone, gets used to cleaning up after himself," he said, brushing her objection aside. "I'll see to the horses."

By the time she was finished and had collected her gear, he had her palomino saddled.

"We're going, Dad!" she called once she was mounted.

From where he knelt in scrutiny of some obscure point of interest, Hastings waved without looking up.

"He'll never miss us." She reined the palomino around.

It took only a matter of minutes to reach the outcropping. Laura noticed that Wayne's eyes seemed never to stop moving. His head was constantly making slight turns this way and that. She recalled his report of the three outlaws camped above them and was suddenly glad of his watchfulness.

He circled the boulders carefully before giving

her the go-ahead to dismount. As she knelt before the face of the rock, he clambered past her to the summit of the highest boulder, rifle in hand. She understood it was so he could command a full view of their surroundings.

She felt the frequent touch of his curious eyes as she set to work on the rock with a stiff brush and a mild acid solution of her father's concoction. With great care she broadened the subject area, applying the brush to clear away the lichens and dirt, then using a rag dipped in the acid to cleanse the stone yet further. Wiping the stone clean with a dry rag, she ran her fingers carefully over it. A little tremor of excitement raced through her.

"Find something?" Wayne's voice from above made her start.

"I think so." She rose to her feet and stepped back to get a fuller view. "Come look!"

He joined her immediately. Even in the excitement of her discovery, she was conscious of his masculine presence close beside her.

"Can you see them?" she asked, with a searching glance up at him.

Wayne studied the rock intently. "Yep. I reckon your dad was right," he agreed after a span of seconds. "You've got yourself quite a find, if I'm any judge."

Laura smiled and turned her own attention back to the stone. Scoured clean by brush and acid, a faint line of characters marched across the yard-wide face of the boulder.

"I'll have to make rubbings of them," she said.

71

"Of course, Dad will still want to come and examine them himself, now that they're fully exposed."

"Are there likely to be more hereabouts?" he asked. She sensed that he too had gotten caught up a little in the compelling excitement of seeking to unearth the mysteries of past ages.

"It's quite possible," she said, pleased by his interest. "Viking runes have been found from Russia to Scotland. The Vikings used them to commemorate significant events, to mark graves, and for magical purposes." She realized she was starting to sound like her father, and fell silent in embarrassment.

"Then let's take a look around," he suggested.

"Okay," she agreed eagerly. "Not all of their writing was done on boulders. Sometimes they worked on smaller stones as well."

"I'll see what I can turn up."

He prowled the area while she fell to examining the remaining boulders in the outcropping. None of them yielded any detectable writings, however, and she broadened the range of her search. She worked downhill, using her boots and a handy branch to scuff aside leaves and the thin layer of topsoil from likely sites.

About twenty yards from the boulders, a small mound caught her attention. As she raked the leaves aside with the branch, she felt the wood scrape on stone. Kneeling, she brushed more leaves away, revealing a flat piece of rock about two feet wide by three feet long. Breathing a little faster, she took the brush to the charcoal gray surface.

She settled back on her knees with a frown when nothing came to light under her strokes. Then she bent closer to peer at the edges of the stone. It was too perfect a rectangle to be natural, and after a few moments she was certain it had been hewn from some larger piece. Ancient chisel marks were still apparent to her trained eye.

Impulsively she dug her fingertips under its edge and tugged upward. The stone didn't budge.

"Need a hand?" Wayne asked from close behind her.

She wondered how he had managed to move so silently in the leaves.

"I need to turn this over. I'm sure it was cut from a larger stone. There might be carvings on the other side."

"We'll see."

He bent to hook his fingers under the stone. Almost effortlessly he lifted it on edge and turned it over.

Once again she used the brush. "Oh, look!" she gasped.

A row of runic characters became clearly visible as the soft loam and debris were cleared from the surface. Wayne knelt beside her as she continued to work. At one point, as the full scope of the carvings became evident, she couldn't resist turning to give him an excited grin. He smiled back, then lowered one callused hand to brush a few remaining bits of dirt away. Briefly she felt his fingertips touch her hand. He didn't seem to notice, and she tried to pretend that she hadn't either.

Then he sat back on his haunches. "Well," he said, "what do you make of it?"

She wasn't sure. Beneath the single row of runes was an elaborate series of carved lines and markings that bore no similarity to any Viking characters she had ever seen.

"I think I'll leave that to Dad," she decided. She cast her eyes uphill, still aware of his closeness and not wanting it to end. "They must've set it up as some sort of marker high up the mountain. Runoff rainwater undercut it so that it fell over. Erosion would've gradually carried it down here. Since it's lying facedown, the carvings have barely deteriorated."

She smiled happily at Wayne. There were noted archaeological professors she knew who couldn't count a find such as this to their credit.

"Congratulations," he said as if he had divined her thoughts. "Another big find, and this one's all yours."

She realized abruptly that his handsome face was scarcely a hand's breadth from hers. The old insecurity, forgotten in the excitement of her discovery, washed over her in a flood. She felt her smile go weak, and she pushed quickly to her feet and stepped back a little.

He rose smoothly. "We can haul it to camp easy enough." He didn't appear to have noticed her unease. "But I reckon your father will want to see it here where we found it before we go to moving it about."

She nodded quickly, grateful for something to say. "That's right. There's still enough time for him to come back this afternoon if we hurry."

When Hastings did return with them, he was noncommittal about the find, although he pored over it for a long time, his brow furrowed in concentration. Once he turned to stare up the mountain as though trying to calculate the original site of the stone. Then he moved to the outcropping and examined it with equal care.

At last he grunted and straightened to his feet. "Perhaps it will become clearer when I've completed my work with the main stone." He spoke in a meditative voice.

Wayne used the pack mule to drag the stone back to their camp. Then, with darkness creeping down the mountain, he rode out for a last check of the area. Laura busied herself with preparations for supper.

"May I visit with you a moment, my dear?"

She was a little surprised to find the professor looming over her. "Of course, Dad."

"Please take a seat." He gestured toward a convenient stone.

Puzzled, she complied. Her pride still smarted a little from his lack of praise over her discovery. He remained standing.

"You did a thoroughly professional job today," he told her.

"Thank you," she said automatically. The belated praise was gratifying, but she knew he hadn't sat her down just to tell her that. "What's wrong, Dad?"

He drew himself up a bit, as though donning the armor of formality. "I couldn't help but notice that a certain, shall we say, familiarity has sprung up rather quickly between you and Mr. Saddler," he began, and she could read the disapproval in his tone.

"What do you mean?" Her voice was a little too sharp.

He would not be rushed. "I have never taken it upon myself to interfere in your personal romantic life," he stated stiffly.

Probably because she'd never had one, Laura thought sardonically, but she held her tongue.

"However," Hastings was continuing, "I feel compelled to state my views regarding your relationship with Mr. Saddler."

"What relationship?" Laura flared despite herself. "Wayne's been a perfect gentleman! And I've never —"

"I am not impugning your morals or your virtue." Hastings cut her off firmly. "Only perhaps, in this instance, your judgment." He paused and regarded her levelly. She bit her lip and remained silent. "I also realize that at this time you have no serious involvement with Mr. Saddler. I am speaking to you in this fashion as a preventive measure."

"What's wrong with Wayne?" Laura could no longer hold back her words.

Hastings pulled in a breath and let it out. "I

have no quarrel with the fashion in which he has done the job for which we employed him. However, I believe those very capabilities illustrate my point."

"What is your point?" Laura demanded tightly.

"Simply this, my dear. Mr. Saddler is little more than a mercenary — a man who lives by hiring out his fighting abilities and his weapons."

"What are you talking about?"

Hastings gritted his teeth in frustration. "Isn't it obvious? Deputy Thomas told us his background. A soldier and then a peace officer — both trades that consist essentially of receiving remuneration for having fighting skills and employing them as directed by others. His very willingness to accept employment as our guide and bodyguard provides another illustration of my point."

"Dad, you all but coerced him to come along with us!" Laura protested. "You offered him a good deal of money, and even said you'd pay for someone to take care of his place while we were gone! You can't blame him for agreeing to come under those circumstances, particularly when Deputy Thomas specifically asked him to do it!"

"The point I am trying to make," Hastings persisted, "is that a mercenary —"

"Quit calling him that!" Now it was she who cut him off. "He's a farmer, remember? He left the cavalry, and he resigned as a deputy!"

"Only to hire on with us," Hastings pointed out smoothly. "If you'll recall, he was involved in a rather brutal street brawl almost immediately."

"He was protecting us!"

"I appreciate that. I merely wish to point out that a man with such propensities will never be satisfied with a farmer's life. Eventually his yearning for violence will surface again, just as it has in the present situation."

So many words and emotions were bubbling up in Laura that she knew if she tried to express them she would manage only an incoherent babble. With an effort both mental and physical, she forced herself to calmness, forced herself to order her thoughts and words in the way the professor himself had taught her.

She clenched her fists tightly and began. "Dad, I hope I would never choose to — to marry someone without your approval. But it's much too soon to be talking about Wayne in those terms."

"Is it?" he asked simply.

"Yes!" she snapped, and immediately wondered if she was lying. She regrouped her thoughts. "I think you're wrong about him. He's not a violent man, unless violence is forced upon him, like it was with that awful Girt. But even if I'm wrong, I'm a grown woman now. You have to realize that. I need to be able to make some decisions for myself."

Hastings stood very stiff and tall. "Very well," he said almost coldly. "We shall leave it at that for the present. I have expressed my opinion. You are, of course, free to do with it as you wish." He turned and strode away into the gathering darkness.

"Dad —" she called after him.

He didn't turn, and she realized with a painful shock that she was glad, because she had no idea what else she could say to him.

CHAPTER 7

The rising sun was behind the far side of the mountain, and the coolness and darkness of the night still clung to the west face as Wayne slipped from the camp. He placed his booted feet silently as he worked his way up out of the canyon and through the trees on the course he had charted the day before. Even with the cover of darkness, he moved like a hunter, keeping to the shelter of woods and shadow.

There was no stir of life behind him in the camp. He had managed to ease from their shared tent without rousing Hastings from his troubled sleep. He wanted there to be no movement or noise to betray the fact that at least one occupant of the camp was awake and astir.

He had sensed a tension between his two charges the night before and wondered what family dispute might have taken place while he had made his evening patrol of the perimeter of the camp. Neither Laura nor her taciturn father had given him any word on it, however; in fact, they had not spoken much at all.

Before turning in, he told them briefly of his plan. "If I'm not here when you get up, don't let on that I'm gone," he finished. "Just act as though I haven't come out of the tent yet."

Laura had watched him with wide eyes, and he had expected her to wish him luck or warn him to be careful. But she had only cut a disturbed glance at her father and remained silent.

He remembered her dark eyes now as he climbed, remembered too the tantalizing sensation of her nearness the day before at the stone outcropping.

She stirred him deeply. He had escorted his share of eligible young ladies from nearby towns to the military balls held at some of the forts where he had been stationed, but none of them had touched him as had this professor's daughter. She would make a good officer's wife.

And what about the wife of a farmer? The question slipped into his mind. He felt a sense of surprise that he was already thinking of her in such terms. He barely knew her at all.

And now was sure not the time for dwelling on her, he told himself, as some humpbacked varmint — maybe a raccoon — ambled out of his path in the gloom.

Wayne wondered what else was aprowl on the mountain. He doubted the mysterious stalker had been watching the camp at night. But if, as he calculated, the man was slinking down from the upper heights to keep an eye on them during the daylight hours, then he wanted to be in a position to get the drop on him if he came this morning.

He hunkered down in a shallow draw that cut across the grade at an angle some hundred yards above the ravine. His position let him look both uphill and down. The ravine was below him to his left.

Hunching his shoulders against the faint chill, he laid the barrel of his Winchester on the lip of the draw and settled down to keep an eye on things himself.

He moved little, listening to the familiar rustlings and callings of the night and striving to pierce the predawn darkness with his eyes. The canyon was lost in the gloom below him.

Gray light eased its way gradually down the mountain. Trees and outcroppings of rock became visible, as did the rim of the canyon, but blackness still cloaked its floor. Even in full daylight, the camp itself couldn't be seen from this height and from this angle. To get a decent look at it, the stalker would need to position himself on the canyon rim, Wayne figured.

He kept an eye cocked at the grade above him. He didn't want to be the one taken by surprise if the stalker was descending stealthily from above.

A shadow darted between the trees on the slope below him. Wayne went taut, then made his muscles ease up. Had he only fancied that he'd seen something move? The grade stretched away, spectral and unearthly in the gray light.

No, the shadow moved again, became a human figure ghosting downward in eerie silence. Wayne turned his head to improve his night vision. The light was still too poor for him to make out details, but in the figure's agile movements he could recognize the same stranger he'd glimpsed disappearing among the rocks the day before.

Abruptly his quarry vanished from view again. Wayne ground his teeth together, then relaxed his jaws as he saw the stalker reappear almost at the rim of the ravine. With hardly a pause his shape melted down into the shadows there. Likely, rather than risk betraying his presence by movement, he would stay right where he was for as long as he cared to watch the camp.

Wayne let several minutes pass. He didn't want to wait too long, for fear daylight might reveal him, but he wanted his prey settled and comfortable before he moved in on him.

At last he eased up out of the draw and started down the grade, using the trees for cover. He didn't know if he moved as silently as the other, but he made it to within about seventy-five feet before he reckoned any farther was pushing the odds.

Standing close beside a tree so his figure would merge with it, he cast a shrewd eye up over his shoulder at the eastern sky. Yellow fire was riding the edge of the mountain. In another couple of minutes the sun would heave into view, and anybody looking upslope would be staring straight into its rays filtering through the trees.

He bided his time. In the building light he could make out a fur-clad figure crouched behind a low ridge on the very lip of the canyon. Two thin objects stuck up like straight horns past his shoulders.

Wayne thought they could be the barrels of a pair of long guns the stranger was carrying strapped across his back.

The mysterious watcher shifted once, as if uncomfortable, and Wayne recalled his own unease at feeling unseen eyes on him. Wayne knew he couldn't risk waiting much longer. This was like stalking a wild animal.

A brilliant finger of light stabbed down the face of the mountain through the trees, illuminating all in its path with glaring clarity. Within moments a veritable flood of light rushed down among the trunks. Wayne didn't look back into the blinding brilliance he could feel behind him. Gingerly he worked the lever of the Winchester, then lifted it to his shoulder. He centered the sights between the rugged shoulders in the animal-hide shirt.

"Freeze, or I'll dig your grave on this mountain!" he said sharply.

The figure jerked slightly, and Wayne could actually sense his target reining in the impulse to turn, as he realized he would be staring directly into the sun while facing uphill under a dead drop. Whoever he was, he was too canny to risk those kinds of odds. He held himself rigid. Only his head turned slightly.

"I always figured this is where I'd be buried anyway," he said in a gruff, raspy voice.

"Your choice whether it's now or later. Raise your hands and stand up so I can see you."

The shaggy figure obeyed. He was tall and ruggedly built, but there was a gauntness to him as well.

"You're the fellow from down in the camp, ain't you?" He spoke over his shoulder again in the same gravelly tones.

"I'm him," Wayne confirmed. "Now, shuck those long guns you're packing."

The stranger shrugged the weapons off his back and held them uplifted, one in each hand, so they were in plain sight. "I'm laying them down gentle-like," he advised. "Had them both for a spell. Hate to see them get banged up by being tossed around."

"Go ahead," Wayne said with grudging admiration.

Carefully, one at a time, the prisoner placed the guns on the leaves underfoot. Wayne could see two other weapons on his belt — a holstered revolver and a sheathed tomahawk.

"Now the six-gun and the throwing ax," he ordered.

Again the stranger obeyed with great care.

"Step clear of them." Wayne moved closer now that the fellow's fangs looked to have been pulled. "Turn around."

Squinting against the sun, the prisoner came about to face him. With a sense of shock, Wayne found himself wondering if he'd somehow slipped three-quarters of a century back in time on this haunted mountain. The stranger he'd brought to bay was the spitting image of an old-time mountain man.

From his obviously handmade animal-hide clothing to his lined and weathered face, grizzled beard, and shaggy, ill-cut mane of hair, he had the look of one of that hardy breed who used to live out their solitary and hazardous lives in the remote reaches of the unexplored West.

Automatically Wayne glanced at the discarded weapons, almost expecting to see an ancient black-powder muzzle loader. But the two long guns consisted of an old Sharps buffalo gun and a long-barreled twin-bore shotgun. Turning his gaze back to their owner, Wayne saw that he'd missed what was probably a small skinning knife sheathed at the mountaineer's waist. He let it go.

"Mighty fine piece of stalking," the stranger's voice cut into his bemusement. "Don't recollect I've ever been outfoxed like that. You was up here waiting for me, weren't you?"

"Yeah," Wayne admitted. "I wanted to know who'd been watching our camp and hanging on our backtrail."

"Shoot, boy, I like to keep an eye on everything that goes on up here on my mountain."

"*Your* mountain?"

His prisoner grinned, showing worn yellow teeth. "That's right. Leastways, I been up here so long I tend to think of it as being my private property." His eyes had adjusted some to the glare of the rising sun. He nodded at Wayne's leveled rifle. "You can stop staring at me down that barrel. If I'd wanted you dead, you'd never have made it up the mountain."

Slowly Wayne brought the Winchester down. "I know," he acknowledged.

The stranger lowered his arms. "I should've figured you'd be up to something like this after the way you veered off the trail looking for me the day you came, and the way you almost hemmed me in yesterday." He shook his grizzled head. "Getting old, I reckon," he said regretfully.

"Who are you?"

The mountain man snorted. "Call me Hawken. Good a name as any. That's the kind of long gun my pa carried."

"Your pa?"

Hawken tossed his head toward the low ridge he'd been using for cover. "Let's settle down if we're going to jaw a bit."

Wayne let out his breath in amazement. He wasn't sure if he'd ever had the upper hand in this face-off. But Hawken had had more than one chance over the past days to send a .50-caliber slug from the old Sharps through him, if he'd been so inclined. And Wayne's instincts urged him to put stock in what the old man said.

Without asking, Hawken knelt to retrieve his weaponry. Wayne didn't try to stop him, but he kept his rifle loosely in his grip.

Gear back in place, Hawken settled himself on the ridge and motioned to Wayne. "Come on, take a load off your feet, boy. Where'd you learn to stalk a man like that, anyway?"

"U.S. Cavalry, and then packing a badge," Wayne answered, amused at the man's brass.

"Pony soldier, huh?" Hawken said flatly. "Never could see my way clear to riding with the boys in blue. Too many rules." His face darkened. "And then I never did cotton to the way they treated the Indians."

There were old emotions buried under the words. Wayne joined Hawken on the makeshift bench.

"You part Indian?" Wayne hazarded a guess.

"Naw." Hawken shook his head. "Married to one, howsomever," he explained. "Pretty little Kiowa gal. Hitched up with her when I was a young pup back in the Rockies. Did it the Indian way, and when I had a chance, I did it right in a church, too."

"You grew up in the Rockies?"

Hawken didn't take offense at the personal nature of the question. "Yep. My pa was a mountaineer. Didn't start out that way, though. When he lost my ma to the lung fever, he closed his store, took me, and headed way up into the mountains. Turned his back on the whole world, I reckon you'd say. He was packing a powerful lot of grief over the way my ma died. Never quite got over it, I guess."

"How old were you?"

"Just a tyke. He raised me up in the mountains. We'd go a whole year without seeing another white man's face except at the big rendezvous each year. Most of my schooling was in hunting and trapping and staying alive. Mainly, my pa had to teach himself, and he passed all his learning on to me."

His first impression hadn't been far wrong, Wayne thought. This was as close to a real mountain man as you'd find nowadays. The rest of his breed had died out years ago.

"Indians finally got Pa. Me and my wife stayed on for a while, but seemed like the mountains was getting full of settlers and miners and all sorts of flatlanders. Her people had been driven out of the region, and eventually they ended up being herded down to these parts by you pony soldiers."

"I recollect my pa telling of seeing action against the tribes," Wayne said coolly.

Hawken studied him from hooded eyes. "Is that a fact?" His tone was grim.

"He always said there was lots of wrongs done on both sides," Wayne went on levelly. "History was against your wife's people. Time to put it all aside now."

Hawken shifted his shoulders as if to work a lingering soreness out of them.

"Likely some wisdom in what your pa said," he admitted gruffly. "Don't make no nevermind now. It's always best to let the old wounds heal. My pa never learned that."

Wayne wondered if his son had. "What happened to your wife?" he asked respectfully.

Exposing Hawken's faded memories and lurking bitterness to the light of day might not be the safest of routes, but he was fascinated by this old throwback.

"We finally came out here to try to live with her tribe on the lands that'd been given to them."

Hawken sighed sadly. "Those were bad times," he went on. "There was lots of sickness and sadness among her people. After a spell of living like that, with neither of us too happy about things, she took the pox and didn't seem like she wanted to get well. She just wasted away.

"Once she was gone, I had nothing to hold me to her tribe. I got my mountain gear together and came up here on this peak. It ain't so much compared to the Rockies — them was real mountains. But this'll do. I've grown right fond of it. I been living like my pa taught me when I was a young'un. I do a little bartering with folks as need be, or go down into the town and trade my furs at the general store." He shrugged indifferently. "Good a life as any, I reckon."

"How long have you been up here?" Wayne asked curiously. The Indian Wars had been over for a good spell.

Hawken gave another uncaring shrug. "Don't much keep track of years no more. Never saw that it made much difference. Like I said when you threw down on me, I plan on dying on this mountain. How long I been up here won't matter then."

Wayne mulled his tale over. In the remote vastness of Poteau Mountain it would have been possible for Hawken to have lived as he claimed. How long had he been here? How long had this strange, lonely hunter haunted this peak? Even in the warming sunlight, a spectral chill touched Wayne for a moment.

"Why's that old fellow and the pretty gal so interested in that rock and them carvings?" Hawken's query intruded on his woolgathering.

"He's a professor. She's his daughter and assistant," Wayne explained. "He thinks the stone might be proof there were Vikings in these parts centuries ago."

"Vikings, huh?" The furrows on Hawken's brow grew deeper. "They're some kind of European tribe, ain't they?"

"Yeah," Wayne told him.

"And the professor thinks they carved them signs on the rock?"

"That's right."

"Never thought I'd see the day a professor would come traipsing up this mount," Hawken said. "Civilization must be getting mighty close. As to who done the carving on that stone, it was already there when I came here. My wife's people had all sorts of writings and signs they used, but weren't none of them anything like what's on that big slab." He paused thoughtfully. "I do know there's some other places on the mountain where there's been similar carvings done."

"I'd be interested in seeing them," Wayne suggested.

Hawken snorted. "Have to think on that a mite. You'd just show them to your professor, and he'd want to stay up here that much longer. Shoot, there's already too many flatlanders on the mountain for my liking."

"Who all might that be?" Wayne inquired without inflection.

"Well, there's those three sorry varmints you spotted yesterday. Hanged if you can't smell their camp halfway up the mountain. If they don't get it in their heads to hightail it out of here right soon, I'm likely to send a few shots their way just so's they'll make up their minds."

"Anybody else?"

Hawken nodded his shaggy head. "Yep. There's another passel of polecats over on the other side of the mountain."

"They led by a fellow in a cavalry uniform?"

"For a fact." Hawken eyed him shrewdly. "You know them, do you?"

Wayne shrugged. "Passing acquaintances. Have they set up to do some mining or prospecting?"

"Mining or prospecting?" Hawken echoed. "Not so's you'd notice. Mostly, they just seem to be loafing."

Wayne frowned. Had Nolen Driver been selling him a bill of goods about his intentions? The ex-soldier had brought his men up here, as he'd said he would, but his purposes for doing it were more murky than ever.

He became aware of Hawken regarding him again. "You think this cavalry hoss might be taking an interest in your professor and his doings?" the mountaineer asked.

"Maybe so," Wayne allowed. "But I can't figure what it would be. His name's Driver. He's got a rep for riding the edge of the law. Where's his camp?"

Hawken described the site, then asked, "You know it?"

Wayne gave a short nod. "Yeah. How many men does he have siding him?"

"Nine, counting himself." Hawken scratched reflectively at his beard. "Looks to be a fighting man. I seen him practicing with his cavalry sword. He's a good hand with it."

Wayne accepted Hawken's appraisal without question. "I'm not surprised," he commented.

Hawken nodded at the bowie sheathed on Wayne's belt. "Can you use that for anything other than whittling?" he gibed.

Wayne grinned a little. "Not much," he said slowly.

Hawken made a snorting sound that bordered on being a laugh. "Let's see it." He extended a gnarled hand.

Wayne hesitated, then slid the big blade free and passed it over, hilt first. He was a little surprised to find himself handing a favored weapon to a man he'd been holding at rifle point not long before.

Hawken hefted the knife like it was nothing new to him. He gazed closely at the keen edge but made no move to test it. Then he grunted as if satisfied and ran his thumb along the brass strip inlaid on the back of the blade.

He grunted again. "You have this special made for yourself, did you?"

"Bought it off the shelf in the general store," Wayne said dryly.

Hawken gave his snorting laugh. "Like thunder you did!"

He bared his worn teeth and shifted the bowie to his left hand. With his right he plucked the iron-bladed tomahawk from his belt.

"Me, I fancy my throwing ax here," he advised.

Then, still seated, he shifted his weight, hiked back his wiry right arm, brought it forward, and let fly in a single flashing movement. The ax whirled through the air like a spinning wagon wheel. Its edge drove deep into wood at the precise juncture of limb and trunk on a sturdy blackjack oak. For a space of seconds the ax stuck there vibrating. Then the two-inch-thick limb sagged slowly away from the tree. Both it and the tomahawk dropped to the ground.

Hawken's grin widened with satisfaction. Still holding the bowie left-handed, he twirled it smartly and offered its hilt back to Wayne.

"Here, you may need to do some whittling."

Wayne felt a grin tugging at his mouth, but he kept his face immobile as he closed his fingers on the bowie's familiar hilt.

The knife wasn't balanced for throwing in the same fashion as Hawken's hand ax. Many a yahoo who fancied himself a knifeman couldn't toss a bowie worth shucks.

Wayne turned slightly where he sat. Twenty feet away an old lightning strike had left a white scar on the trunk of another oak. Extending out in front of it from a nearby tree was a forked branch as thick as his wrist, just the kind of obstacle that, struck glancingly, could divert a thrown knife from its target.

Wayne gripped the hilt of the bowie firmly and cocked his arm. Then, smooth and fast, he whipped his arm forward. End over end, the whirling bowie flashed in the glimmering sunbeams. Like the stroke of an ax, its honed edge hewed through the branch in passing. The tip buried itself in the white lightning scar before the severed branch touched the ground.

"Not much besides whittling," Wayne drawled.

Hawken emitted a bark of laughter and clapped him solidly on the shoulder. "You'll do to winter with, Pony Soldier! What name are you packing?"

Wayne told him.

"Well met, Wayne Saddler." Hawken shoved out his callused hand and clapped Wayne on the shoulder again as they shook.

Rising, Hawken crossed to retrieve the bowie and his tomahawk. He turned back with the knife balanced in his right hand.

"Here's your whittling tool." He grinned and flipped it spinning high overhead.

Wayne didn't move. The bowie reached the height of its arc and dropped. It sank halfway to its hilt in the soil a scant pair of inches from the toe of his boot. Hawken's eyes lit up with obvious pleasure at his accomplishment.

Casually Wayne plucked the knife from the

ground. He doubted he could match that stunt with Hawken's tomahawk. He hoped he'd never have to cross steel with the mountaineer.

As Hawken came striding back, Wayne twisted about to look down toward the camp. He saw Laura kneeling beside the cookfire, her hair black and glossy in a stray beam of sunlight. The professor stood with hands on hips, staring at the giant rune stone in silent contemplation, as if seeking to wrest its secrets from it by sheer force of will.

"Come on down to the camp," Wayne invited. "The professor and his daughter would admire to meet you."

Hawken's seamed face darkened some. "Reckon not," he said. "I ain't too much for socializing with their sort. Ain't much for socializing at all, far as that goes. I've jawed more with you than with anyone I can recollect in years."

With his knowledge of the mountain, Hawken would be a font of information for the professor. But he wasn't a man to be pushed.

Wayne shrugged. "It's a standing invite," he promised.

The idea of getting together with flatlanders seemed to have dimmed Hawken's enjoyment of his meeting with Wayne. He hitched his shoulders to get the two long guns riding comfortably, then weighed his tomahawk in one big hand.

"Glad you never had to fight my wife's people, Pony Soldier," he said gruffly.

"So am I," Wayne told him honestly.

Hawken grunted wordlessly and slid the ax back

into its sheath. "Might look you up again before you ride out," he said, then grinned. "I'll be sure you don't see me coming next time."

Wayne matched his grin. "Keep your gun barrels clean."

"Always."

Hawken swung around and strode away. Within only a matter of seconds his tall, gaunt form had disappeared in the woods, fading away in the shadows and sunlight. So might Jim Bridger or Jed Smith or others of the legendary mountain men have moved, Wayne mused.

He watched for a moment longer, but there was no further trace of Hawken's existence. Shaking his head in wonderment, Wayne turned to make his way back to the camp.

CHAPTER 8

"I've got it!" Professor Trevor Hastings addressed himself with great satisfaction. He leaned back in his chair and exhaled. "I should've grasped it long before now."

In front of him, on the folding camp table where he habitually worked in his tent, were the notes and transcriptions that had gone into his translation of the rune stone's characters. After considerable effort and numerous false starts, he had unlocked a mystery kept in this remote canyon for centuries. The implications were staggering, not only for the understanding of the history of this continent, but for the vindication of his own theories as well.

Eagerness and excitement welled inside him. He rose, the sheet bearing the final translation gripped tightly in his hand, and ducked from the tent into the early-evening dusk.

"Laura!" he called, elation in his voice.

"What is it, Dad?" Laura came hurrying from the fire.

He saw Saddler turn in their direction from where he tended the horses. "You too, Mr. Saddler!" He gestured peremptorily.

Wayne left the horses and came striding over.

"You look like a man who has achieved his goal,

Professor," Wayne said, smiling.

"In a sense I have, Mr. Saddler. I've succeeded in translating the runes," he announced formally. "There can be no question. They are undeniably of Viking origin."

"Oh, Dad! That's wonderful!" Laura clapped her hands together.

Saddler grinned a bit at her happiness before turning an interested gaze back to Hastings. "Congratulations, Professor."

"Tell us about it, Dad!" Laura urged.

"Very well." Hastings squared his shoulders. Already he was envisioning himself addressing future audiences of scholars and students.

"As you are aware," he began, "I copied the characters faithfully as the first step to deciphering them. From the outset, I was puzzled by them. They appeared to be of runic nature, yet only two of them, the second and the last, matched letters of the Scandinavian Futhark, the alphabet most commonly used, as you know, Laura, by the Scandinavian peoples in the ninth century. That was the period in which I have estimated their landings on this continent took place. However, the remaining characters did not fit that alphabet. Even allowing for the writer's errors or illiteracy, all possible translations resulted simply in gibberish."

Hastings paused to assess the reaction of his audience. Laura was listening raptly. Wayne looked intrigued by the account.

"I was completely baffled and was beginning to believe that the carvings were nothing more than

99

a random work by some ancient North American stone carver, which resembled certain letters of the Scandinavian Futhark by coincidence. Naturally, I was extremely discomfited by this conclusion."

Hastings lifted the paper in his hand and displayed it dramatically. "Then it dawned on me that, while the characters did not match the Scandinavian Futhark, there was more than a passing similarity to the Germanic, or Old Norse Futhark, of which I have also made a study. When I used the Old Norse as a basis for translation, I observed that, with the exception of minor irregularities easily accounted for by weathering or the individual hand of the carver, the runes conveyed a quite legible message."

"But, Dad," Laura interjected, "the Old Norse was used as far back as the fourth century. That's much earlier than anyone believed the Vikings could have reached this continent!"

Hastings was pleased at her quick grasp of his discovery's ramifications. "Quite so," he said. "Either the carver was deliberately using an antiquated style of writing for reasons of his own, or the Vikings had actually penetrated virtually to the center of this continent by the fourth or fifth century."

"What do the characters say, Professor?" Wayne asked.

"Translated to Latin, they read GLOME DAL," Hastings announced, "which means 'Valley owned by Glome.' Apparently the stone was meant as a marker or warning that this canyon was the property of a Viking, likely a chieftain, named Glome."

"That implies more than just an exploration party passing this way," Laura said with dawning comprehension. "It could mean Glome and his followers actually lived here for a significant period of time, perhaps even established a settlement."

"Correct," he agreed.

"Dad, I'm so proud of you!" She stepped forward, and he accepted her congratulatory hug.

"Isn't it exciting, Wayne?" She turned her attention to the ex-lawman, beaming up at him.

"Of course, it means significantly more work," Hastings said stiffly before Wayne could respond to her. "We must attempt to locate the site of a possible settlement in this region."

"Much chance of that after thirteen hundred years?" Wayne asked skeptically.

Hastings gestured dramatically at the giant rune stone. "This marker survived. Perhaps other traces and artifacts did also."

"Like the other stone, and the carving on the outcropping!" Laura pointed out enthusiastically. "Dad, you must try to translate them as soon as possible!"

"In due time." Hastings had his own theories about the smaller stone Laura had uncovered.

In her excitement, Laura reached out and gripped Wayne's arm with both hands. When she saw her father's face tense up she released her hold.

"We shall lay out our plans for proceeding with

work here tomorrow morning," Hastings stated curtly, then turned to walk to his tent.

"Yes, Dad." Laura's tone was sober.

The soft sound of a footfall, the impression of movement outside the tent, snapped Wayne's senses alert out of a restless sleep. Automatically his hand sought the Colt in its holster beside his bedroll. He eased it clear of leather and lay for a moment longer, listening.

Across the tent Hastings snored quietly. The horses weren't kicking up a fuss, but Wayne was sure something untoward had roused him.

Silently he slipped from his bedroll and, crouching, peered out of the front of the tent. Wan moonlight filtered through the trees and cast objects in shades of black and white and gray. He could smell the faint scent of spruce trees.

It took him a moment to discern the pale, slender figure of Laura Hastings standing at the edge of the camp, looking out into the darkness. She wore a long white gown or robe, and had her arms wrapped tightly about herself. The ebony mane of her hair fell loose to her shoulders, dark and luxuriant in the moonlight. Wayne caught his breath at her beauty.

Then, as she continued to stand gazing into darkness, solitary and immobile, he felt a frown of concern pull at the muscles of his face. Taking care not to disturb her father, he tugged on his boots, stuck his pistol under the belt of his jeans, and slipped out of the tent.

Deliberately he scuffed his boots against the ground so she would hear his approach. Even so, she turned sharply with a little gasp.

"Oh!" she exclaimed softly. "It's you. I'm sorry if I disturbed you. I couldn't sleep."

"It's no problem," he assured her quietly. His own sleep had been uneasy. Unremembered dreams and strange thoughts hovering at the edge of wakefulness had kept him from getting much rest.

"I saw you out here and wondered if you were all right," he added.

He couldn't read the look she gave him, but he fancied it might almost have been one of fear. Surely that was only the poor light, he decided. She didn't answer him immediately but turned her gaze back out to the darkness.

Hesitantly he moved to stand beside her, staying at arm's length, wary of having his intentions misunderstood. He thought she shivered a little, but she didn't draw away from him. The long flannel nightgown she wore shifted with the slight movements of her body beneath it.

"Big day for your father," Wayne tried for a response.

She nodded somberly; then, as though realizing something more in the way of a reply was called for, she added aloud, "Our findings will vindicate his theories if they're accepted by his colleagues."

"Is there any question of it?"

She shrugged. "There's always a question when

it comes to changing accepted beliefs and concepts among scientists."

Her heart didn't seem to be in the conversation, but he didn't want to let her return to that remote, forlorn silence. "The translation using the older runic alphabet will confirm all he says, won't it?" he persisted.

"That's the trouble. Dad's one of the few men qualified to handle translations from the Old Norse alphabet. He's done a special study of it." She turned her head to glance at him. "We'd never have made this find without you." She looked away before he could catch her expression.

"I'm sure we'll find more evidence to back up his theories," he offered awkwardly.

"Do you think that strange old man you told us about will be willing to help us look?"

"Hawken?" Wayne frowned. "Hard to say which way he'll jump. By most folks' standards, he's a mite loco."

"But not by yours?" she asked with an odd intensity.

"I don't know," Wayne answered honestly. "I reckon I understand how he felt when he shucked it all and came up here to live. Been times when I felt like doing that same thing myself."

"Why didn't you?"

Her eyes were warm pieces of onyx in her pale face, and Wayne met their compelling gaze. "Maybe I figured I'd eventually find the right person to share things with me. I was always afraid to give up and quit looking."

Without warning she jerked her head sharply around. A visible shiver raced over her.

"I'm scared, too," she said so softly he barely caught her words.

"Of being up here on the mountain?" he asked blankly.

She shook her head slightly. The long waves of her hair rippled in the moonlight. "No," her voice was still quiet. "I'm scared of not finding someone. But I'm almost as scared of what happens if I do."

"It's called falling in love," Wayne said hoarsely.

"Have you ever been in love?" she asked timorously, without turning her head.

"I reckon I'm mighty close right now."

Wayne reached for her and turned her gently toward him. He didn't know how they'd come to this point, but he could no longer deny the feelings welling up within him. He could sense the warmth of her skin through the cloth of her gown. She didn't resist his touch, but her body was stiff and straight.

"There's no need to be afraid of me, Laura," he said, and drew her to him.

For a moment she did resist, and then abruptly she came against him in a rush, her lips pressing his in a brief, fumbling kiss. Then she ducked her head away, and he felt her strain backward against his arms. Instantly he let go.

"I'm sorry —" he began awkwardly, but she only shook her head fiercely.

"It's not you!" she cried. "It's not your fault,

and I'm not scared of you!" She dodged past him and fled toward her tent.

Nonplussed, Wayne stood and stared after her, wondering if he'd finally found something precious only to lose it, all in the same handful of moments.

CHAPTER 9

"Hello, the fort!"

The voice rolled out of the woods at the mouth of the ravine. Wayne came to his feet from where he'd been sitting near the cookfire. In the gray of early dusk the trees were a dark wall that his eyes couldn't penetrate.

Laura had also straightened, skillet forgotten in her hand. Wayne felt her dark eyes on him, fearful and questioning. Near the rune stone, Hastings was peering into the woods with a frown on his aristocratic features.

"Get over there with your dad," Wayne ordered Laura. "Stay under cover until we see who it is."

In the back of his mind the voice and the greeting had echoed with a familiar ring. He took two strides and snatched up his Winchester where it leaned against a stump. At waist level, he swung its barrel to bear on the canyon mouth.

"Ride in easy!" he shouted. "Show me your hands!"

"Yes, sir!" the familiar voice came back with a twang of mockery.

Wayne had the sudden impulse to glance over at Laura to be sure she was safe. He kept his eyes on the woods. Since that moment the night before when he'd held her briefly in his arms and felt the touch of her lips on his, he didn't think her image had left his mind's eye for an instant.

She'd been cool and aloof through the day, and there was no chance for him to make amends for whatever trespass he'd committed. Fact is, he wasn't sure what had happened between them or why she'd fled his embrace. Perplexity and confusion had ridden him like an ornery cowhand on a mustang.

He'd spent a good part of the day patrolling the area of the camp. On the occasions when he saw Laura, the professor was keeping her busy with his painstaking survey of the canyon floor. Using shovels, brushes, and picks they were seeking to uncover traces of a Viking settlement. The scars of their efforts showed here and there under the trees.

The professor's manner, too, had been almost hostile. Wayne didn't know why Hastings had been on the prod the last couple of days, either. He had a notion it was something to do with his interest in Laura. But since both father and daughter seemed bent on not talking, he didn't figure he was going to be enlightened anytime soon.

"Coming in!" The visitor's voice was closer now.

Wayne left the trail of his thoughts about the professor and his daughter. He wasn't too surprised to identify the mounted figure that hove into view from the cover of the trees.

Nolen Driver sat his big Appaloosa like he rode

at the head of a column on dress parade before a visiting general. The scabbard of his cavalry saber protruded from beneath the tail of his duster, and his left hand rested on its hilt.

He looked to be alone. No other horsemen appeared out of the gloom behind him. His white teeth flashed in a grin beneath his full mustache as he saw Wayne's stance.

"No need for a call to arms," he advised easily. "No hostiles in the vicnity."

Wayne realized that with Girt Tannery's knowledge of the mountain at his command, Driver wouldn't have had any trouble learning the location of the canyon. But what did he want here?

"Thought I'd see how you folks were coming along," Driver said as if in answer to Wayne's unspoken question. "You're the closest I've got to neighbors up here and, truth to tell, keeping company with those fellows riding under me gets a mite tiresome after a while."

Whatever Driver was after, he didn't seem overtly threatening. The ex-soldier wasn't fool enough to ride in under the enemy's gun if he was planning to commence hostilities.

Wayne set the rifle aside. "Step down," he invited.

Driver executed a flawless dismount. With well-trained patience his horse stood where he left it.

"Ah, there are your compatriots." Driver had spotted Hastings and Laura moving out of the shelter of the rune stone. "I don't believe I've had the pleasure of meeting either of them formally."

Tersely Wayne made introductions. Driver clasped the professor's hand and looked him squarely in the eye. He performed a precise military bow to Laura that put to shame Wayne's effort when he'd first met her. Both father and daughter were reserved in their responses.

"I'll see to supper." Laura started toward the fire but drew up with a brief questioning glance at Wayne.

"Driver will join us," Wayne told her. Maybe over dinner he could pry some answers from their visitor.

"I'm sure I'll appreciate your cooking after the camp fare I've been having, Miss Hastings," Driver said, accepting with easy grace.

Laura smiled politely. "I'll get the three of you some coffee while you wait."

Driver might never have made the rank of officer, Wayne mused during the meal, but he played the role mighty well. By turns he was courteous, charming, and witty with his hosts.

"An excellent meal. My compliments, Miss Hastings," he said as he settled back with another cup of coffee.

She nodded acknowledgment.

Wayne still didn't have a notion why Driver had paid them this visit. Could be, he supposed, the man really did just want some company other than that of gunsels and hard cases.

"How's prospecting?" Wayne asked aloud.

Driver snorted derisively. "All we've done so far is sit on our tails and wait for Girt to show

110

us his big strike. He claims he can't locate it again now that we're here. Spends lots of time prowling around while the rest of us just loaf. My men are starting to get their bellies full of the whole deal."

"Wouldn't be the first time a mine or cave has disappeared up here, according to the tales," Wayne commented. "Seems it's sometimes hard to locate the same spot twice on the mountain, since so much of it looks alike."

"Is that a fact?" Driver put his cup down and got a cheroot going.

"Well, I'm about at the end of my tether with Girt," he continued. "If he can't show us some color in the next few days, I'm sending him packing, and good riddance." He shook his head ruefully. "We came all prepared to mine that strike. We packed up everything from picks to dynamite. None of it is much use now."

Driver's words matched what Hawken had told him, Wayne recollected. "Girt's been known for selling a stray steer now and again," he said.

"If he's sold me one, he'll regret it." Driver drew hard on his cheroot, and for a moment, in the firelight, his face wasn't that of a gentleman at all. He speared the thin cigar sharply into the fire. "Riding command on a pack of hard cases, and dealing with the likes of Girt Tannery," he said broodingly. "Ain't like the old days, serving under the crossed sabers, is it, Saddler?"

"Some different," Wayne allowed.

"You miss it though, don't you?" Driver demanded with a dark intensity.

111

Wayne shrugged. "Not so much."

Driver recoiled like a striking rattler that had bumped its snout. "You're telling me you don't hanker for the sound of the bugle, the feel of the wind in your face when you make a charge, the satisfaction of standing side-by-side against the enemy?"

"There was that," Wayne conceded. "But mostly I recall bad food, cold quarters, low pay, long hours in the saddle, and the risk of catching a bullet from an outlaw or from some recruit who couldn't handle a gun."

Driver frowned in puzzlement. "That why you quit?"

"Mostly." Wayne's mind roved back over those days of violent action offset by mind-numbing tedium, of fleeting glory and endless drudgery. "My pa saw I went to West Point. He expected me to serve a hitch when I got out, and I figured I owed that to him, even though he was dead by then." Wayne hiked his shoulders. "I didn't mind doing it for a spell, but when my time was up, I was ready to move on."

Wayne became conscious that Hastings was watching him intently from across the fire. The professor's face was as hard to read as that of the rune stone.

"What rank were you?" Driver probed. Wayne's words seemed to have pricked him in some dark way.

"I made captain."

Driver stared into the fire. "Never got past ser-

112

geant major myself," he said bleakly, and Wayne guessed suddenly that it wasn't an admission the man made often. "Of course, I never had no West Point education, either," Driver went on. "I aimed to go higher than sergeant major, but it didn't work out. The big brass never could see the enlisted man's side of it, never could see that sometimes the rules just didn't work when dealing with the enemy." Bitterness rode his tones.

Wayne held his peace. He recalled Heck Thomas telling of Driver's drunken murder of a reservation Indian. Driver was nursing a grudge, clinging to a past that had become more wish and fancy than hard reality.

Driver lifted his eyes from the glare of the fire. "You might be right, though," he said. "You and I missed the glory days, back during the Indian Wars. Tracking the Apaches across the desert and running them to ground, taking on the Comanches on horseback and beating them at their own game, fighting hand-to-hand and matching sword against tomahawk!" His voice rose as he spoke, and his fingers curled around the hilt of his saber. "Those were the days that bred real heroes, men like George Forsyth, John Chivington, General Custer."

An odd collection, Wayne noted. Steadfast and courageous, Major George Forsyth, commanding fifty soldiers, had held off a combined force of six hundred Sioux, Cheyenne, and Arapaho warriors on a sand dune known as Beecher Island. Brutal and fanatical, Colonel John Chivington had slaughtered a village of women, children, and oldsters of Chief Black Kettle's tribe. And Custer, vainglorious and power hungry, had led his troops blindly into disaster at the hands of the Sioux.

"Forsyth may have been a hero," Wayne said deliberately. "But Chivington was a butcher, and Custer was a fool."

Driver's eyes flared ominously. "You disappoint me, Captain," he said in clipped tones. "You've been listening to the wrong accounts of history, accounts written by Easterners and greenhorns who've never been west of the Mississippi. If it had been left to weaklings like them, the West would've never been tamed!"

There was no gain in prodding him further, Wayne figured. "Either way you cut it, the old days are dying."

Some of the tension eased out of Driver. His shoulders sagged a bit. "There's the truth of it," he said bleakly. "Another twenty years — shoot, another ten — there won't be any place left for men like you and me. The greenhorns and weaklings will be running everything."

Wayne thought of Hawken and his flight to the mountain to avoid the encroachment of civilization. Was he himself like Hawken and Driver, a relic of an earlier, more violent time?

He shook off the thought. He had put his days of battles and showdowns behind him, and laid his hand to the plow. Unlike Hawken and Driver, he'd made his peace with the past. The West was almost tamed now, for all that Hawken and Driver and even he might regret its passing. Maybe that was for the best.

"What the deuce," Driver said abruptly. "Come what the devil gives me, I'll still make my way. I'll blaze my own trail. Like the Vikings! Right, Professor?"

Hastings regarded him as if examining some strange new artifact and remained silent.

Driver gave an almost sneering grin. When he reached to pluck a burning brand from the fire the glow made his face look almost feral. He rose, strode away from the fire, and halted before the towering mass of the rune stone. He raised the torch until the line of runes was illumined in the uncertain light.

"So this is it," he said without looking around. For a long span of seconds he stared at the enigmatic characters. Then he shook his head as if in frustration. "Can you read this, Professor?"

"Given time," Hastings said casually.

"You haven't deciphered it yet?" Driver demanded without taking his eyes off the runes. "You don't know what it says?"

"I'm working on it."

Laura was watching her father intently. She was plainly curious about his reluctance to discuss his discovery.

Driver wheeled around from his study of the stone. Standing there, his torch upraised, his duster like a cape, his sword at his side, he cut a barbaric figure.

"Why do you think those Vikings were here, Professor?"

"Exploring, perhaps," Hastings answered.

"They were raiders and outlaws, weren't they?" Driver pressed. "Like the desperadoes of the old days here. Free-living men! Didn't they raid and loot wherever they went?"

"They were a warlike people," Hastings conceded. "But mostly they were seafarers and explorers."

"I've read how they pillaged entire regions," Driver insisted.

"Frequently they raided coastal areas," Hastings replied patiently, as he might have spoken to an argumentative student in a university class.

"What did they do with all their loot, their treasure?" Driver's eyes shone in the light of the torch.

"Much of their loot, as you call it, was on the order of foodstuffs and perishables. They also took captives and used them as thralls. What they had in the way of treasure was lost over the ages as they eventually became peaceful traders instead of pirates."

The hungry glitter faded from Driver's eyes. "Civilization conquered them, too," he muttered. Then his voice took on strength once again. "But they were heroes in their day!"

"That's certainly not the way I think of them," Laura cut in firmly.

Driver bared his teeth in his sneering smile. "Of course. This is hardly a pleasant topic for after-dinner conversation, particularly following the fine meal you prepared." He returned to the fireside. "My apologies, Miss Hastings."

She gave a small nod of acceptance.

Driver tossed the brand back in the fire with a swordsman's flick of the wrist. Sparks erupted, then winked out of existence. Dropping a hand to the hilt of his saber, Driver looked to be posing as he glanced up at the stars beginning to light the night sky.

"Getting late," he announced. "I need to be riding out. I've enjoyed the hospitality of your camp." This time the smile he bestowed on them was utterly charming. "Do I have your permission to call again, Miss Hastings?"

"Please do," Laura responded with little enthusiasm.

Driver turned a questioning gaze on Wayne. "No objections from a fellow soldier, I trust?"

It was better to have a man like Driver where you could see him, Wayne thought. "Free range in these parts," he said.

"Excellent. Good evening, Professor."

He pivoted smartly on his heel and stalked to his horse. Vaulting into the saddle, he wheeled his mount and snapped a crisp salute at Wayne.

Almost despite himself, Wayne used a forefinger to return it.

Smiling as if he'd won some victory, Driver reined the Appaloosa about and took it out of the camp at a canter. In moments the centaurlike figure disappeared among the trees.

"Keep talking like I'm still here," Wayne whispered to the professor and Laura.

He was moving toward the heavier woods at the mouth of the ravine before either of them could reply. Behind him he heard their voices, hesitant at first, then more assured as they went along with his ruse. Without looking back he headed into the trees.

He didn't know what kind of game Driver was playing, but he wanted to be sure the ex-soldier wasn't still lurking in the vicinity of the camp. Once in the shelter of the thicker growth, he paused and listened. Up ahead sounded the rustle of a horse's hooves among leaves. Driver wasn't making any effort to conceal his whereabouts. If need be, a good cavalryman could move his horse through the leaves with all the stealth of a cougar.

Wayne pressed forward. In the gloom the trees were spectral shapes that reached for him with cold, fleshless fingers. He imagined the restless spirit of the ancient Viking Glome, prowling through these woods he once had claimed as his own.

Pale white flickered through the trees ahead. Wayne drew up short, then realized he was seeing only the shifting folds of Driver's duster as the horseman moved out of the mouth of the canyon. By the time Wayne reached the spot, Driver was just a ghostly white shape fading into the darkness downhill. In moments he had disappeared altogether.

Frowning, Wayne crouched there for a spell. At last he straightened and turned back toward the camp. As he did, a shadow slid behind a thick bole on his right. Wayne's hand swept his Colt from leather, the hammer coming to full cock with a metallic click.

"Easy, Pony Soldier." The shadow moved again, took form as a familiar rugged figure. "Mite jumpy, ain't you?" Hawken asked dryly.

Slowly Wayne let his thumb ease the hammer down. "Must be our night for visitors," he said just as dryly.

Hawken grunted. "Saw that Driver fellow riding in. What'd he want?"

Wayne wondered why the old mountain man figured it was any of his concern. "Just some company, to hear him tell it," he answered anyway.

Hawken glanced after Driver. "Wears that sword and uniform like he was still in the cavalry," he grumbled scornfully.

"Maybe he thinks he is."

Hawken spat. "Seen his type before. He's nothing but a hard case, a flatlander. Only reason his kind come up here is to stay clear of the law, or to plot trouble."

Wayne holstered the Colt. "He's not wanted by the law around here."

"Maybe not, but mark my words, he's out for no good."

Wayne shrugged. "Long as he minds his manners, I don't much care what he's doing up here."

"Just the same, you guard your backside, Pony Soldier."

"You still watching our camp?"

119

Hawken stiffened a little at something in Wayne's tone. "I done told you already, I like to know what's going on up here on my mountain."

Wayne jerked his head back in the direction of the camp. "Come on in and meet the professor and his daughter," he offered. Hawken's motives were as murky to him as those of Driver. He wanted the elusive mountaineer where he could keep an eye on him.

Hawken backed off a step. "Reckon I'll think on that a spell." He hesitated, then added gruffly, "You and me got a few things in common. Don't know as how I can say the same when it comes to a professor and a pretty young gal like that."

Genuine or not, the declaration was a rough gesture toward friendship. "Do me a favor then," Wayne requested.

"What is it?" Hawken asked with immediate suspicion.

"Let me know what Driver and his pack are up to."

Hawken seemed to chew the idea over. "Reckon as how I might do that," he allowed finally.

It was as much of a commitment as he was likely to get, Wayne figured. "Obliged."

"I'll give some thought to meeting the professor and his young'un," Hawken promised roughly.

Before Wayne could come up with a response, Hawken wheeled away. Even watching him, Wayne couldn't be quite sure how he managed to fade into the darkness within a handful of strides. No sounds followed his leaving. Wayne imagined he felt a cold breeze wend its way into the canyon. He glanced back once, then headed toward the fire.

Laura and her father were engaged in some sort of close talk, which they broke off as he arrived. She took a step toward him.

"We were worried." Her eyes were wide. "Did he leave? Did you see anything?"

"He's gone." Wayne didn't mention Hawken's shadowy presence in the woods.

"I need to clean up after dinner." Laura swung about and hurried off, as if leery of prolonging the conversation.

Hastings looked to have been waiting his turn. He studied Wayne shrewdly. "I heard what you said about your military service," he stated flatly. "If you didn't enjoy such work, why did you become a lawman?"

Wayne blinked in surprise at the question. Everybody seemed to be catching him when he wasn't looking this evening.

"Tracking lawbreakers was something I knew how to do from my hitch in the cavalry," he explained, not trying to keep the puzzlement from his voice. "Being a deputy gave me a chance to earn a little money, and to get to know the Territory better before I settled down."

The professor's features were again unreadable. "And why did you quit the marshal's office?"

"So I could settle down." Wayne corralled his impatience with the older man's odd queries.

"I'd had my fill of getting paid for how well I pulled a trigger or handled a blade," he elaborated. And that was about as much of an answer as he was willing to give any man, he decided.

Hastings mulled his words over, looked as if he wanted to probe further, then apparently changed his mind. Without saying anything more, he marched off toward the tent.

"Professor," Wayne called after him.

Hastings halted rigidly. "Yes," he answered, coming halfway back around.

"I reckon I'll be sleeping outside of the tent from here on. That way I can keep watch on things better. I'll bed down a little ways off from the camp. Thought I'd let you know."

"Very well," Hastings said crisply. "Do as you think best." He resumed his advance on the tent.

Shaking his head, Wayne went to see to the horses. He questioned silently whether Hawken was watching the camp at this very moment. Or had he faded away through the night to whatever obscure den he had made his lair?

Laura was still cleaning up the dishes when he finished his chores. She straightened as he drew near.

"I heard what you told Dad about sleeping outside," she said. The subject seemed to embarrass her. "Does that mean there's more danger now?" She stepped closer to him but seemed to be unconscious of doing so.

"Not really," Wayne replied. "I just think it'd be a good idea."

He didn't add that with Driver now having paid a call on them, Hawken still hanging around, and who knew what or who else skulking about, his own presence on the outskirts of the camp would make it harder for them to be taken by surprise at night.

Laura appeared to accept his explanation, but she didn't seem too anxious to end their conversation. She dried her hands and said, "I didn't care for Mr. Driver."

"He's lonely and bitter," Wayne said, surprising himself a little at coming to the ex-soldier's defense.

Laura's eyes widened. "You sound like he's your friend!"

Wayne shook his head. "He's no friend."

"Well, I wish he hadn't come here."

Wayne wished the same, but with her standing so close to him, and the moonlight casting her features in pale ivory, Nolen Driver and his doings were suddenly the furthest thing from his mind. He remembered the feel of her in his arms, the warmth of flannel beneath his palms, the brief, tantalizing press of her lips against his.

"I never meant for you to take offense last night," he told her. His tone was colder than he would have liked. She stiffened at his words. "You don't have to apologize," she said with fierce intensity. "Not for anything!" She wheeled and ran to her tent.

Tiredly, Wayne went to get his bedroll. He recalled the advice Hawken had given him. It did seem like a good idea to check behind him just before he bedded down.

CHAPTER 10

Hawken crouched in the brush and watched the tattered buckskinned figure go by. Of all the men riding under Driver, this one had the best makings of a mountaineer. He moved quietly enough, and he was a passable woodsman. If it hadn't been for the stench of his clothes and body, Hawken might not have been able to detect his approach in time to seek cover.

The sorry varmint liked to prowl the vicinity of Driver's camp, Hawken knew from his past secretive observations. Driver also kept sentries posted in good military fashion, although they were easy to avoid if a man knew what he was doing.

As the woodsman passed from view, Hawken left his concealment and slipped forward. The morning sun was high enough to send beams shooting down through the leaves and branches to dapple the ground in shadow and light. Hawken stayed to the shadows, moving with the stealth and cunning that his father had taught and that long ago had become second nature to him.

Driver had made his camp in an easily defensible hollow half encircled by low rocky walls. Silently Hawken worked his way in amid the brush and rocks above the camp to a point where he could peer down at its occupants. Before he settled himself, he spared a searching look up the wooded grade behind him, recalling how neatly Wayne Saddler had outfoxed him. But his practiced eyes could detect no lurking dangers, and he turned his attention to the camp.

It had been his grudging commitment to the pony soldier the night before that had brought him here this morning. He was a little bewildered with himself for agreeing to keep an eye on Driver.

It had been long years — how many he couldn't calculate — since he'd had anyone he could rightly call a friend. Truth was, he'd never been much in the way of a sociable man. His lonely upbringing had had something to do with that. Most of his life had been lived in solitude, and since he'd come to this mountain — *his* mountain — he'd seen less and less need to have any contact with other folks.

If Wayne hadn't gotten the drop on him so efficiently, he likely would have left the professor's party alone to finish their strange work and depart from the mountain. Such was the pattern he had fallen into over the years — watching the comings and goings of flatlanders on the mountain and letting his presence be known to them only when he needed to do some bartering.

Most who came to these remote slopes were renegades and owlhoots like the three outlaws hiding out above Wayne's camp. Hawken despised their breed, but he let them go their way unharmed so long as they didn't intrude greatly on his solitary life.

How much longer could that type of life last? he wondered. Things were mighty different now than they'd been when he was a young'un. Back in those days a good part of the country had been almost empty of people. The Indian tribes had, for the most part, been easy enough to get along with if you treated them with a measure of respect. They had gone their way, and mountain men like his father had gone theirs.

But these days everything was different. Now there were only a few lost places, like this mountain, that weren't overrun by civilized folks. And more and more flatlanders were finding their way even up here for one reason or another. It was a sorry day when an Eastern professor showed up to do some researching on an old rock that had been on the mountain since long before Hawken himself had come.

Not that the professor and his pretty daughter were bad folk. They were a sight better than most of those who came to these parts. And from the first, Hawken had felt an odd kinship with their hard-edged guide. The pony soldier could have survived in the mountains back during the old days, Hawken reckoned.

He shifted his position slightly and felt the pain in his joints that hadn't been there a few years ago. Age was creeping up on him like civilization was creeping up the mountain.

Driver's voice, giving commands, rose from the camp. The ex-soldier was issuing his morning's orders, assigning what paltry duties there were for the camp, and sending out new sentries. All of the men obeyed readily enough, although their actions fell some short of military snap and precision.

"Yes, sir, Captain," one hard case drawled as he sauntered off.

Driver watched with satisfaction as his orders were carried out. The men not chosen for duty continued to lounge lazily about. As a military camp, it left a sight to be desired, Hawken observed contemptuously.

Driver turned and stalked back into the tent, which served as his headquarters. It was the only tent in the camp. Driver's men bedded down beneath ramshackle lean-tos or under a large rocky overhang. It was still a puzzle to Hawken what Driver figured he was doing here.

In a moment the commander reappeared from his tent. He was stripped to the waist, and the blade of the sword he carried caught a shaft of sunlight so that for a moment he seemed to hold a saber of fire.

Standing sideways, left hand on his hip, sword presented to some imaginary foe, Driver assumed a bent-kneed stance. None of the hard-bitten men looking on spoke a word. There were no jeers or catcalls. That alone said something, Hawken figured, about the respect in which these tough men held Driver and his odd weapon.

Driver swished the blade in some sort of swordsman's salute, then began a series of cuts, lunges, and parries that might have been a drill he'd learned in the cavalry. Hawken noted the smooth roll and play of the muscles in the ex-soldier's bare chest and arms. Driver didn't look soft, he conceded grudgingly.

He kept watching as Driver increased the speed and complexity of his movements. Some of it Hawken had seen when he'd spied on the camp before, but it was still quite a sight. He didn't know much about swordfighting, but he was better than passing fair with a knife, and he suspected Driver was a mighty good swordhand.

A whisper of sound or the movement of air warned Hawken. His attention distracted by Driver's performance, he'd been careless, he realized instantly. Someone or something was close to him and moving his way.

Hawken held himself rigid, barely daring to breathe. Whatever was approaching didn't seem to know he was there. If he stayed still and didn't make a sound and maybe even prayed a little, he might go undetected.

He strained his ears and flicked his eyes over as much area as he could manage without turning his head. He did let his hand creep, ever so slowly, toward the tomahawk at his belt. Best to keep this silent if it came to bloodletting.

A faint whiff of foulness brushed his nostrils. It was the buckskinned loner. Upwind of him, Hawken hadn't caught his scent in time. The fellow was moving past the thicket where Hawken crouched, scant feet away.

Hawken remembered the soreness in his joints and wondered whether he'd be able to move fast enough if he were discovered. It was a new thought to him. He had relied on his own abilities for so long that the idea they might fail him was unnerving.

But the faint sounds of the woodsman's movements went by the thicket. Turning his head a notch, Hawken saw his ragged figure. As his eyes touched him the fellow hesitated in his gliding stride. Immediately Hawken dropped his gaze to the ground. After a pair of seconds he sensed the other pass on.

Only then did Hawken risk lifting his eyes again to study him. This one had the makings of a mountaineer, right enough. Hawken saw the big knife on his belt and he was willing to wager that the fellow was more than passing fair with it.

Hawken began to breathe more regularly. That had been close. One way or another, he should have sensed the man's return. With a pack like this, he couldn't get careless. If he did, then his grave might be up here on the mountain a lot sooner than he'd planned.

He peered at the bivouac as the woodsman entered it and strode up to Driver, stopping just out of range of the flashing sword. Driver made a few more passes with the blade, then halted. He was breathing heavily, and sweat gleamed on his torso. He cocked his head and listened as the woodsman spoke to him in low, emphatic tones. Hawken couldn't catch the words. Once the fellow gripped the hilt of his knife suggestively.

Driver nodded, as though in agreement. "We

won't wait much longer," his words reached Hawken's ears.

Driver used his saber to gesture toward his tent in invitation. The woodsman took him up on the offer. Hawken thought he glimpsed a look of distaste on Driver's face before the ex-soldier followed him into the tent.

What to make of that? Hawken questioned silently. If Driver was really doing some prospecting — and this was the sorriest bunch of prospectors Hawken had ever seen — then apparently he'd just about had his fill of it.

Wayne Saddler might be interested in that news, and Hawken felt like he'd ridden his luck far enough for today in watching the hardcase camp.

Stealthily he withdrew from the thicket. Once clear of the sentries, he headed toward the other side of the mountain, where Wayne Saddler had his encampment.

"Oh!" Laura cried softly.

Wayne came about from where he'd just stood the small rune stone erect beside its larger brother. Laura was back near the spring, cleaning some stone fragments her father had unearthed. Her gaze was fixed on the gaunt, rugged form that had just emerged from the trees at the mouth of the ravine. Relaxing a bit, Wayne went to meet their visitor.

"You're getting right careless, Pony Soldier," Hawken cackled as he approached.

"A man could get shot sneaking up on a camp thataway," Wayne replied sardonically.

"You'd have to see him, first." Hawken showed his worn teeth in a gleeful grin.

"Glad you decided to accept my invite."

Hawken started to answer, then looked past Wayne and blanched. For a moment Wayne thought he might turn and bolt back into the forest like a wild animal.

"Who's our guest, Wayne?" Laura had drawn near.

From the look on Hawken's leathery face, Wayne figured the mountain man would likely rather be facing a brace of owlhoots with only his tomahawk than be standing where he was right then. As he turned to make introductions, he saw Hastings striding toward them from the small excavation where he'd been working. The professor's head was cocked quizzically.

"Laura, this is Hawken. I've told you about him." Wayne presented the young woman.

"My pleasure, Mr. Hawken." Smiling, Laura stepped forward. "I'll be fixing supper shortly. You're welcome to join us."

Hawken gulped visibly, then seemed to gather his resolve. "Shoot, missy, don't need no 'mister' on my name. Just Hawken is fine. And, by thunder, if you ain't the prettiest thing to come down the pike in a long spell!"

"Why, thank you." Laura beamed at him.

Hawken was getting over his shyness awful fast, Wayne noted.

"Mr. Saddler says you know these mountains better than any man living," Hastings said without preamble as he reached Laura's side. "An honor to have you in our camp." He extended a work-hardened hand.

He had chosen the right approach. Hawken clasped the offered hand. "And I reckon I'm right honored to be here," he allowed gruffly.

After that the mountaineer seemed to make himself at home. In moments Laura had them served with tin mugs of sweetened tea, still cool from the spring. Hawken smacked his lips appreciatively and let the professor draw him over to the rune stone, where he recounted his first view of it years before.

"I done thought I was seeing things, stumbling upon it the way I did," he recalled aloud. "Then I realized it was the same stone the Indians talked about."

"What do they think of it?" Hastings asked with interest.

Hawken shrugged fur-clad shoulders. "Most figure it's bad medicine and stay clear of this ravine. Some say evil spirits done the carving; others reckon it was the mound builders that used to live in these parts."

"Mound builders?" Hastings queried.

"Indian burial mounds," Wayne supplied. "At least, that's what most folks figure they are. East of here there are several good-sized mounds. If you dig into them, you turn up pieces of pottery, fragments of masonry, and human bones.

No one knows who left them or what purpose they served."

"Curious," Hastings commented thoughtfully. Briefly he seemed distracted by this new mystery. But nothing could draw his interest away from the Vikings and their travels for long. "Are there any other stones like this on the mountain?" He indicated the giant block.

Hawken grew reticent, as if sensing he might be asked to take up the role of guide. "Nothing much," he mumbled.

Wisely, Hastings backed off the subject a little. "If you do come across any, I'd very much like to see them. I'm certain there is other evidence of Vikings' having been here. They had to have had dwellings, since there are no caves on the mountain —"

Hawken cocked an eye. "Oh, there's a cave, right enough."

The professor's shoulders stiffened. "Are you certain? Where is it?"

"Don't know for sure," Hawken muttered.

"What do you mean?" Hastings asked.

Hawken shifted his weight uncomfortably and glanced in Wayne's direction. Wayne was a bit puzzled as well.

Hawken muttered something to himself. "Ain't never told nobody this before."

"Please tell us." Laura had drawn near just in time to hear the tail end of what had been said.

Hawken gave in with surly grace. "When I come up here after my wife died, I had a dog," he began.

"Little thing — not much more than a pup. Brought it with me from my wife's village. I figured I'd be needing some company." He shook his head. "When I lost him, it hurt durn near as much as losing my wife, or seemed to, anyway. Figured then and there I was going to have to get along by myself, and I have ever since."

"What does this have to do with a cave?" Hastings asked bluntly.

Hawken fixed him with a gimlet stare. "Got everything to do with it," he growled. Old and painful memories echoed in his tone.

Hastings relented. "Go on," he said encouragingly.

"Me and the pup was learning our way around the mountain one afternoon when he got all het up as if he'd caught the scent of some varmint. He took off like a shot into a thicket under a ledge. He was barking to beat all, and there was a commotion in the thicket. Then it seemed like his barking started getting further and further away. And there was a funny kind of echo to it.

"I poked into the brush and found sort of a wall of rocks that'd crumbled away in one place. Looked old, mighty old. The hole in it opened into some kind of cave, and my pup had gone through it after whatever varmint he was chasing. I looked in, but couldn't see nothing except blackness. Smelled kind of musty. I took to calling the pup, but I just kept hearing his barking get fainter and fainter. Finally it stopped altogether." Hawken fell silent and stared blankly at the rune stone as if seeking some answer from it.

"You never found your dog?" Laura asked sadly.

Hawken shook his grizzled head. "Never seen him again. He went in that cave and plumb disappeared. Still in there, far as I know. Or likely just his bones after this long."

"But you said you don't know where the cave is located?" Hastings asked.

"I don't. I kept calling the pup for a while, and when he didn't come out I figured I was just going to have to go in after him. The hole was too small for me to squeeze through, so I headed back to my camp to get a pickax so's I could widen it." He scowled at his memories. "Got in too big of a hurry, I reckon. My camp was halfway to the other side of the mountain, and I wanted to get the pickax and make it back before it got too dark to work. Anyway, I was fixing to cross a crevice, rather than going around it, and I slipped and fell a good dozen feet. Hit my head when I landed. Dang fool thing to do. I still got the scar." He probed his shaggy mane of hair with a blunt finger.

"Don't know how long I was out. It was morning when I came to, so it could've just been overnight — could've been longer. I was all banged up and didn't recollect much of what'd happened right then. I made it back to my camp and passed out a second time. When I woke up I remembered the pup. I got my pickax and tried to make it back to the cave." Sadness brooded in his eyes. "Couldn't find it. One thicket under an overhang looks pretty much like another on this mountain, and my recollections was never real clear after hitting my head thataway."

Had Hawken imagined the whole tale? Wayne asked himself. Or had he, subconsciously, never wanted to find the cave again because of the pain of his loss?

He cut a glance at Hastings to see how he was taking the mountaineer's account. The professor was studying Hawken with a curious intensity. Wayne remembered his earlier doubts about there being any caves on the mountain.

"You have no idea on which side of the mountain the cave was located?" Hastings said finally.

Hawken moved his head slowly back and forth. "I looked high and low for a spell, but never found it again. I finally gave up. Don't really matter, though. Nobody's ever going to know all the secrets of this mountain, no-how."

Strangely, Hastings didn't seem inclined to question him further. The professor's expression was thoughtful as he stared at the two rune stones.

"You will stay for supper, won't you, Hawken?" Laura stepped smoothly into the gap.

Hawken started, then looked down at the tin mug in his hand as if he'd forgotten it. Telling the story appeared to have summoned up old demons to torment him. He looked ready to flee even this remote outpost of civilization.

"Reckon not, missy," he said without any more explanation.

Laura retreated a hesitant step. "You're welcome anytime," she told him with evident sincerity.

Hawken seemed not to hear. He swung his shaggy head toward Wayne. "That flatlander and his pack was talking about riding out," he advised gruffly. "Thought you ought to know."

"Thanks." Wayne hesitated. Laura had withdrawn toward the fire; Hastings was still preoccupied with the stones. "Sorry about the pup," Wayne said.

"I still miss him now and again," Hawken remarked absently. "Never wanted another one. I figured, if I got one, something would just happen to him, too." He blinked a couple of times then looked over his shoulder at Laura and her father. "You folks will do to ride the river with," he said. His tone was still gruff.

Wayne knew better than to acknowledge the rough compliment. He moved with Hawken toward the edge of the campsite.

"So long, Pony Soldier." There was a note of finality in his voice.

Wayne gave a slow nod. "Keep your guns loaded for bear."

"Been doing that for years. Don't figure to quit now."

Hawken swung about and headed into the woods. Wayne let him go. He fancied the old man was moving with a slight limp. For a moment he turned his eyes away, and when he looked again, Hawken was gone.

"Will he come back?" Laura had left the fire

and joined him. Her voice was troubled.

Long shadows were beginning to stretch across the canyon floor. "I don't know," Wayne replied.

Laura shivered and hugged herself tightly. Wayne got the sudden feeling that she wanted to move closer, but she glanced in her father's direction and stayed where she was.

"That poor man," she murmured. "And his poor dog." She turned soft dark eyes up at Wayne. "Do you believe him?"

"Yeah."

The stark image of the bones of a long-dead dog lying in a forgotten cave flashed in his mind. He remembered Hawken's comment about the secrets of the mountain and wondered what other dark mysteries it held.

CHAPTER 11

Nolen Driver reined his horse in and cupped a hand to his mouth. "Hello, the fort!" he bawled.

"You getting lonesome for company again?" Wayne drawled, stepping out from behind the tree that had shielded him.

Driver twisted sharply in his saddle, reaching automatically for his pistol.

"Easy," Wayne cautioned. He kept his own hand near his holstered Colt.

"You move like a blasted Indian," Driver said sourly. "Where'd you learn that?"

"We had a couple of Cherokee scouts assigned to us in the cavalry. I made it a point to learn everything they could teach me."

Driver relaxed a little. His grin looked a bit forced. "I was wanting some more good cooking," he explained affably enough. "Thought if I showed up about now, I might get leftovers from breakfast."

"That's up to the cook." Wayne gestured toward the camp in wary invitation.

"You had my back up there for a minute," Driver commented grudgingly as he moved his horse forward at a walk.

On foot, Wayne fell in alongside, careful to stay

140

clear of the range of Driver's booted foot. He still didn't trust the man, but he felt a grim kinship between them, one born of battlefields and the scent of gunsmoke. He wasn't sure he liked the feeling.

Moodiness had dogged him since Hawken had recounted the haunting tale of his lost dog the evening before. He had been prowling the perimeters of the camp when he'd heard Driver's horse. The ex-soldier hadn't been trying to hide his approach.

"How much longer you figure to play at being a prospector?" Wayne inquired casually.

"Not long, I can tell you," Driver said emphatically. He used a forefinger to tip back the brim of his cavalry hat. "Your professor about finished looking at old rocks and such?"

Wayne shrugged. "I reckon he could take a month of Sundays and still not be satisfied."

"Has he found anything worth keeping?" Driver's tone was casual, but he sat his horse rigid as a sword blade. His fist was gripping the reins in a stranglehold.

"Nothing to speak of," Wayne told him.

Driver eased up a bit. His horse tossed its head and let out a short whinny.

From the woods at their backs, another horse answered. The sound was quickly cut off.

Wayne's head snapped around to meet Driver's shrewd stare. "One of yours?" Wayne asked flatly.

Driver shook his head tightly. "I'm riding alone."

Wayne believed him. All in an instant, Driver

141

had become taut as a stretched strand of barbed wire. He wasn't lying about being surprised.

"Then we got company."

"Maybe the two of us better have a look-see," Driver suggested tersely.

That suited Wayne. Whoever was out there was likely an enemy. He didn't cotton to leaving Driver behind him while he went to check it out.

"We'll split up," Driver decided. "Catch them between us."

Wayne didn't have any argument with the plan. He nodded.

"Hey, Saddler?" Driver's grin was fierce.

"Yeah?"

"Remember Captain Chaffee's command when he was leading his men against the Kiowas? He told 'em, 'Forward! If any man is killed, I will make him a corporal!' " Grinning, he wheeled his horse away in eerie silence.

Wayne didn't wait to see him go. He catfooted forward, watching and listening as he moved. With only the two of them, it would be easy to miss the enemy entirely in the forest.

In the shadow of a looming trunk he paused to palm his Colt. The woods were still and quiet. He could hear his heart pumping within his chest and made himself listen beyond that. Of Driver there was no trace. Had he misjudged the man? Was Driver stalking him?

Wayne shooed the thought aside and moved on, swinging wide before he cut back toward the canyon's broad mouth.

With no warning a wild cavalry yell tore through the air. A pair of shots answered it. Crouched low, Wayne legged it in the direction of the sounds.

A pair of figures came dodging through the trees ahead of him. Wayne drew up short. He had only a heartbeat to recognize Shooter, the lean outlaw from the camp up the mountain. Shooter had a six-gun in each fist and was flanked by his cohort, Pete. In the same instant the pair spotted him and skidded to a halt. Both the guns in Shooter's hands came up and spat flame.

By the flick of a snake's tongue, Wayne fired first, cocking and triggering twice so fast the two reports merged as one. Shooter jerked like a puppet, both his six-shooters pumping lead into the ground at his feet.

Wayne dropped to one knee and heard Pete's first bullet whip-crack close overhead. Through a haze of gunsmoke he lined the Colt on Pete's dim figure and fired twice more before the owlhoot could trigger again. Pete spun about and went down.

Wayne stayed in his crouch, pistol leveled in his fist. Gunsmoke teared his eyes. He had two shots left, but neither of the hard cases moved. Most men didn't after taking a pair of .45s in the chest.

Still cautious, Wayne came to his feet. The third outlaw, Zeb, was still unaccounted for. Then, over the chiming in his ears, he heard an exultant shout and the unmistakable clash of steel on steel.

He stalked swiftly forward, thumbing new shells

into the cylinder by feel. As the last cartridge slid into place, he came out on a small clearing that served just fine as an arena for mortal combat.

The final outlaw, Zeb, was in a knife fighter's crouch, his rusted machete jutting up from his fist. Facing him, Driver stood in a fencing stance, sword presented to his opponent. A small smile curled his lips beneath his mustache. Zeb was panting hard, and sweat gleamed on his face. Plainly there'd already been more than one passage of arms.

From the side of his vision, Zeb must have glimpsed Wayne because, with the odds against him doubled, he yelled an oath and sprang on the offensive, wielding the machete in savage slashing strokes. Casually, Driver retreated before the barrage of steel, using his wrist to flick the saber in short, controlled parries.

Wayne felt his muscles go taut. Driver was toying with his opponent like a cougar with a rabbit. Against the ex-soldier's longer blade and practiced skill, Zeb's wild attack didn't have a chance.

Then, as Zeb's arm began to falter beneath the machete's weight, Driver stood his ground and made one final parry. The tip of the saber moved in a tight, blurring circle. The machete was wrenched neatly from Zeb's grasping hand. It spun away.

Zeb stood stricken, his face just beginning to show shock and horror. Driver gave him a clock's tick to let his awareness grow, then leaned into a long, driving lunge. The tail of his duster snapped out behind him with the speed of his movement. The cavalry sword pierced Zeb's chest.

For a long, frozen instant Driver held his stance with Zeb transfixed on his saber. Then he hauled the blade free and recoiled into an on-guard position as Zeb toppled to the ground.

Wayne didn't holster his Colt. He held it loosely at his side as he went forward. Driver whipped around to face him, then lowered his sword. The ex-soldier's teeth were bared in something like a grin. His nostrils flared wide as he breathed.

"The others?" Driver demanded eagerly.

Wayne jerked his head over his shoulder. "Back yonder," he advised tersely.

"Dead?"

"Yeah."

Driver's grin widened. "By thunder, we made them sound retreat, didn't we?"

"One way of putting it," Wayne agreed without inflection.

Driver sneered at Zeb's lifeless body in epitaph. He flicked his gaze back to Wayne. "Who the devil were they?"

"Some wanted men who had a hideout up the mountain a ways."

"They were sneaking up to the camp, on foot, when I spotted them and mounted a charge," Driver explained. "They scattered like heathens, and I dismounted to engage them. This one wanted to play with cold steel. I obliged him. Their horses must be tied further out." Driver made little fencing motions with the tip of his blade where he held it, point down, at his side. Wayne doubted he was even aware of the movements.

"They must've been leaving the mountain when they spotted you or got wind of the camp," Wayne surmised aloud. "Then they decided to come see what they could find."

"I had the feeling for a minute that somebody was sniffing on my backtrail, but I didn't see nothing. Coming after me, all they got was a taste of lead and steel!"

Wayne was fed up with his boasting. "Reckon the professor and his daughter will be fretting," he said. "They'll have heard the commotion."

"Mr. Saddler! Shout if you can hear me!" the imperious voice of Trevor Hastings rang out from the direction of the camp as if to confirm Wayne's words.

"Coming in!" he hollered in answer. Wayne hesitated. Brutal though his methods had been, Driver had helped him successfully fend off what could have been a deadly attack on their encampment. He owed the man a little hospitality for that. "I'm not alone!"

Driver strode over and picked up something from the ground. Wayne saw that it was Zeb's rust-pitted machete. Driver balanced it in his left hand against the saber in his right. Then he sheathed the sword and deftly switched the machete to his right hand.

"Spoils of battle," he said with another grin. "I think I'll hang on to it. My horse is over here."

With his grim souvenir in his fist, he went to

146

the Appaloosa and stepped up into the saddle. Wayne holstered his Colt and glanced ruefully at Zeb's body. There were some graves to be dug, and some words to be spoken over them.

Tiredly he turned to accompany Driver.

No one was in sight when they emerged into the ravine. Driver reined up, peering about alertly. Then Professor Hastings stepped into view from the cover of the rune stone, his big foreign-made hunting rifle cradled in his arms. A moment later Laura appeared with her Winchester from behind the tent.

Wayne felt a sense of satisfaction. Calling out like Hastings had done was a tenderfoot's move, but he and his daughter had been ready for trouble nonetheless.

As she saw Wayne was unharmed, Laura set her rifle aside and came to him in a rush. Of a sudden he was holding her, feeling her hug him tightly in relief.

"Oh, praise heaven," she gasped. "When I heard those shots and saw you were gone, I thought —" She drew away from him, embarrassed.

"What happened out there?" the professor demanded as he drew near. He still carried his big game rifle.

Wayne answered him tersely.

Driver dismounted smoothly. "We put them to rout, Professor," he advised as he joined Wayne. "It would've done your heart proud to see it!"

"I doubt that," Hastings said.

Driver had already turned to Wayne. "Have you

ever used a sword in combat, Saddler?"

"A time or two," Wayne replied tonelessly.

He wasn't lying, but, by and large, the cavalry saber had never been of much use in warfare. It was worn mainly for show in ceremonies and routinely left behind by most soldiers while on patrol.

"There's nothing that equals matching cold steel with an enemy," Driver enthused. "When I was in the cavalry, I was fencing champion of every base where I served."

"Congratulations," Wayne said dryly.

Driver eyed him curiously. He didn't seem to notice the way Laura and her father were regarding him.

"You don't sound like a man who's just won a major victory, Captain," he said to Wayne.

"There's nothing to feel good about," Wayne told him flatly. "Killing's just a dirty job that sometimes has to be done. I started farming because I wanted to be finished with battles and showdowns."

"No wonder you quit wearing the blue, Saddler," Driver said in wonder. "You don't understand what the cavalry is all about. There's honor in combat, and personal fulfillment in seeing your enemy go down under your weapon."

"Well, then you got some today, I reckon." Wayne didn't see any reason for debating. He turned to Laura before Driver had time to retort. "I could use some coffee."

"Of course." Her face was flushed. "I'll get it."

Wayne felt her father's intense gaze on him. He ignored it.

"That's a fancy rifle, Professor." Driver had taken note of the double-bore Rigby. "You any good with it?"

"I've used it on occasion," Hastings said stiffly.

"Care for a little shooting contest? I'd like to try it out." A calculating gleam appeared in Driver's eyes.

"There's been enough gunplay for this morning," Hastings advised him coldly.

Driver busied himself getting out a cheroot. His eyes were hooded beneath the brim of his hat. "Maybe you're right, Professor," he acknowledged when he had the thin cigar lit. He wheeled and strode to his horse. Atop it, he leveled his cheroot at Wayne. "I'd like to have seen you in action, Saddler."

"Maybe you'll get a chance yet," Wayne said.

Driver smiled without much warmth. "Yeah, maybe I will. Give Miss Hastings my regards. I suppose sampling her cooking again will have to wait." He clamped the cigar back between his teeth and snapped his flattened hand to his forehead in a crisp salute.

Wayne didn't return it.

Driver's smile grew thinner. He didn't look back as he rode out.

CHAPTER 12

Professor Trevor Hastings drew a deep breath as he watched Nolen Driver leave the encampment. He had no regrets at the hard case's departure.

"A brutal man," he commented. "He obviously enjoys violence."

Wayne glanced around at him. "Yeah," he agreed shortly. "Seeing him use his sword wasn't pretty."

"I believe I owe you an apology, sir," Hastings said.

"An apology?"

"I have misjudged you, and I have spoken ill of you. I would ask that you accept my apology."

Wayne stared at him with puzzlement written on his chiseled features. "I don't know what you've got to apologize about," he said finally, "but I'm not bearing any grudges."

"Thank you, Mr. Saddler."

"If you meant all that, start calling me Wayne."

"Very well, Wayne." Hastings found himself appraising the big ex-officer in a new light. He liked what he saw, he realized.

The traits of strength, courage, and resolve had been there all along in Wayne Saddler. The professor had simply misread them in view of the man's background as a soldier and a lawman. But seeing Wayne's distress over having killed two men who undoubtedly deserved killing, and his cold contempt for Driver, who reveled in the bloodshed, Hastings knew he had been mistaken. Wayne could be a hard man, and he was strong enough to do what had to be done, but he wasn't without compassion.

Hastings had righted one wrong. That still left the hardest part of his task: Now he had to talk to Laura.

"Here's your coffee, Wayne," her voice intruded on the professor's reverie. She handed Wayne a tin mug. "Dad, did you want some?"

Plainly, she was puzzled by the expressions of the two men. "Ah, no thanks, dear," Hastings answered her a little vaguely.

"I'm glad that man's gone," she said with a shiver. "I didn't want to come back over here until he was."

"I hope he's gone for good." Wayne drank his coffee, wincing at the heat. "Thanks." He practically shoved the cup back into Laura's hands. "I'm going to saddle up."

"Where are you going?" Laura asked quickly.

Wayne paused long enough to answer. "I aim to follow Driver and see if I can figure out what he's up to. You both will be safe enough here so long as you don't venture out of the canyon."

"Be careful," she said.

"Don't fret." Wayne headed for his horse.

Hastings thought he caught a quick disapproving

look from his daughter before she turned away. He lifted a hand and started to call her back, then closed his mouth and let his hand fall back to his side. Best to wait until Wayne was absent from the camp.

He sighed as he watched Laura return to the fire to finish her duties. She was an attractive young woman, he acknowledged with some pride. He had done his best to raise her, but he understood now that he had fallen woefully short in some respects. Dragging a growing girl from campus to campus and from one archaeological dig to another as the demands and whims of his career dictated may have been adequate to provide her with an excellent education, but it had hardly been sufficient to prepare her for adult life in other ways.

He knew she had had few, if any, serious beaus. The matter had never particularly disturbed him. On the contrary, he had been secretly pleased not to have to deal with that aspect of raising a daughter. But now that the issue had finally arisen in this unlikely setting, he found himself quite inadequate to handle it.

Not that his concerns over Wayne Saddler's perceived character defects hadn't been perfectly proper under the circumstances, he reassured himself. A father had every right to look after his daughter's interests, especially when it came to matters of this nature. But his approach had been boorish and dictatorial, both traits that he had taught Laura to disdain. His behavior had caused a rift between them that he would bridge today if he could.

He still had some doubts about Wayne's suitability as a beau for Laura. For all his attributes, the man was still a farmer — hardly the sort of companion he would have chosen for his daughter. But it was not his choice to make, he reminded himself.

With grudging relief he saw Wayne ride out of the canyon on Driver's trail. Laura was kneeling by the fire, still busy with cleaning up after the morning meal.

There was no point in delaying this any longer. But it would have been far easier to face a roomful of critical colleagues than to do what had to be done now. He offered up a little prayer for strength and went firmly to do his duty.

Laura tensed as she saw her father approaching. She had hoped he would go back to his painstaking survey of the ravine floor and leave her alone.

She was saddened by the barrier that had grown so swiftly between them. But her burgeoning feelings for Wayne left her helpless to surmount it.

The knowledge of Wayne's feelings toward her was at once exciting and terrifying. His attempt at an apology the other night had almost broken her heart. Certainly he had nothing for which to apologize. It was her father's stubborn blindness and her own paralyzing fears that were to blame for keeping them apart.

She noticed that her father's stride was determined. No doubt he had taken note of the impulsive way she had hugged Wayne and was now prepared to deliver another stilted lecture on Wayne's supposed shortcomings.

She set her mouth firmly and told herself she would not react to whatever he had to say. He was, after all, her father and had a right to express his views.

Oddly, his determined stride faltered slightly. He halted and drew himself up in that manner she knew so well. Mentally, she braced herself.

"Yes, Dad?" She glanced up briefly, then dropped her eyes back to her work.

"There is a matter between us which must be resolved."

Inwardly she cringed. Was he going to forbid her even to speak with Wayne? How could he do such a thing? And what would be her reaction if he did?

"I believe I have erred in my perceptions of Mr. Saddler, or, rather, Wayne."

For a few seconds she was sure her ears had betrayed her. She looked up sharply, then rose trembling to her feet.

"What do you mean?" she managed with a mouth gone suddenly dry.

Hastings actually cleared his throat. She had never before seen him so nervous.

"I have done an injustice to our guide, by assuming him to be a man drawn to violence. After observing him and listening to his words, I can

154

see that such is not the case."

"Oh, Dad —" Laura gasped.

His uplifted hand forestalled any further outburst. "Allow me to finish," he requested firmly, then marched steadily on. "In light of this, I must retract many of the recent remarks I made to you concerning his character." He hemmed and hawed a bit more, then gathered himself a final time. "Well, I would have no objection to his, ah, paying court to you, if that is your wish."

"Bless you!" Laura could be constrained no longer. She reached out to him and was overjoyed to have him return the hug. "Thank you, Dad," she murmured against his shoulder.

He released her a little awkwardly. She brushed away a tear and said, "I never meant to hurt you, Dad."

"Nor I you." He was smiling at her joy. Then a trace of his sternness returned. "This is not to say that I am giving you license to behave in any sort of inappropriate manner. My primary desire, of course, is for you to be happy. If Wayne Saddler can make you happy, then you have my blessings."

"I don't even know if he's really serious," Laura heard herself protest halfheartedly.

Hastings smiled. "I'm sure you'll have any doubts resolved before too long, my dear."

Laura hugged him again; this time she clung to him tightly.

Driver hadn't made any effort to conceal his tracks, Wayne quickly realized. From Hawken's description he knew the approximate location of his quarry's bivouac. He was certain he had passed by the spot once before on the trail of outlaws during his days as a peace officer.

Driver had ridden steadily, without sidetracking or doubling back. Wayne was careful to keep an eye out for the telltale flash of white from Driver's duster. He didn't want to ride up on the man unexpectedly, and he was determined to get a look at Driver's bivouac.

Seeing Driver's bloodthirsty skill with his treasured blade had only proven his conclusions that the ex-soldier was a dangerous man and one who would bear watching. But if Driver meant to harm him or the Hastingses, why had he sided with them against the three outlaws?

No reason — except, perhaps, Driver's own fevered desire for action and violence.

When he was still a good ways out from the hollow that Hawken had described, Wayne swung from his saddle and slid his Winchester out of its scabbard. He left the paint tied and muzzled in a brush-choked draw, then went ahead on foot.

Wayne expected that Driver would have lookouts on patrol. But even given that his men were seasoned gunhands, Wayne doubted they had the discipline to make good sentries. They probably only tolerated the duty out of respect or fear of their commander.

He estimated he was still over a hundred yards from the encampment when he found what he was seeking. An ancient crack in the side of the mountain had eroded into a shallow depression. He eased down the rocky slope, cautious of loose stone sliding beneath his boots and of rattlers that might be lurking in brush at the bottom.

Standing upright, he could peer over the lip of the rift. Setting his hat and rifle aside, he squinted down through the trees. He couldn't see into the hollow, and its stone walls would serve to muffle sounds. Then the faint scents of woodsmoke and coffee wafted to him on a breeze. He had found the bivouac right enough. Now he had to locate the sentries.

He settled in to wait and watch. The day was well along. The sun was tracking across the blue sky above the leafy branches. A trio of squirrels came down from an oak to squabble and search for acorns. Wayne watched them with half an eye, trying not to let their antics distract him.

When one of them stiffened and sat up high on its haunches to peer downslope, he paid them more heed. Abruptly all three of them scrambled frantically back up the oak, their bushy tails flicking in alarm.

Wayne directed his gaze in the direction he'd seen the first one look. It took him a moment before he made out a lone figure trudging along amid the trees, rifle carried carelessly at his side.

Wayne watched until the inept guard wended his way out of sight in the woods. The boldest of the squirrels scampered down out of the oak and resumed its scrounging. It was safe to move. Left-handed, Wayne reached for his hat.

Unexpectedly the squirrel snapped bolt upright and stared past him with wide eyes. It had seen something to alarm it.

Wayne wheeled around in a crouch, his right hand taking his Colt, his thumb earing back its hammer, all in the same whipping movement. Reflex and training brought the barrel in line with the buckskinned Girt Tannery, who stood thirty feet away, a rifle raised to his shoulder. Out prowling, Girt must have spotted him and sneaked up on him like an Indian to get a sure shot.

Wayne locked his finger before it could pull the trigger. He was staring into death. Behind the unwavering barrel of the rifle, the lean, stubbled face of Girt Tannery snarled back at him. Girt, too, held his fire.

"Make your first shot good, Saddler," Girt growled, "because I'm taking you with me." The rifle barrel was dead steady. Girt wasn't going to back down.

Wayne's mind raced like a spurred horse. Even on the off chance that he survived a shoot-out with Girt, the gunplay would betray his presence to Driver and the rest of his pack. He didn't want that; not yet. Either way this played out, he stacked up to lose.

So, he had to make it a new game.

"Listen to me, Girt," he said tersely. "I got a way we can settle this."

"I'm listening."

Wayne kept his gun leveled. He resisted the urge to moisten his dry lips. "You're packing your bowie. So am I. We almost crossed steel before. You willing to finish it now?"

Girt bared his fangs in a slow, ugly grin. "I'm willing, Saddler." His voice was gritty as a rattler's warning. "It'd pleasure me a heap to carve you up."

Deliberately Wayne lowered the hammer on his Colt. "Then shuck your rifle and come ahead," he invited coldly.

CHAPTER 13

"I been hankering for this, Saddler," Girt growled.

Wayne didn't answer. Girt's big bowie was in his right fist, the arm tucked close to his body, his left arm extended a little bit to guard. He moved the same way he had back in town, catlike and wary, circling to his right. His moccasined feet were almost silent on the uneven footing of the grade.

Wayne's stance and movements matched him like a mirror image. He watched everything about his opponent, not concentrating on the eyes, or the feet, or the constantly feinting blade. When Girt attacked for real, his whole body would go into the effort.

"Your prettied-up blade ain't going to help you none," Girt jeered, noting again the brass inlay along the back of Wayne's knife.

"We'll see," Wayne said.

Girt answered with a wide sweep of his knife that fell short of Wayne's middle. Wayne wasn't fooled. Wide slashes left a man's body open to a return thrust. They were the stuff of amateurs and greenhorns. Girt was neither.

As his circling carried him above Wayne on the slope, he struck for real, slashing in a tight arc at Wayne's face, sliding his right foot forward into the move. Wayne jerked back, catching only a glimpse of the big blade as it flashed past his eyes. He went in under Girt's arm and lunged at his midriff.

Girt dodged clear, outside of Wayne's blade. His slash came like a snake's strike at Wayne's knife arm. It was a pro's move, aimed at Wayne's right side, his dangerous side. Wayne twisted away from it, swinging his own blade up and out to counter. He felt Girt's bowie clash against his, far too close for comfort. Girt's blade was battered aside.

Wayne teetered on the slope. He cut at Girt, but the stroke was too wide. Girt came over it with another slash at his face. Wayne sprang awkwardly away.

Girt had the edge now. He fancied those tight cuts at head and face, and he kept coming. To protect his eyes, Wayne gave ground and regained his footing, but he had no chance to do anything save shift his own blade to block and parry Girt's unrelenting attack.

Steel gleamed in front of his eyes. The clash of metal chimed in his ears. One missed block, one slow parry, and he would be disfigured or blinded and, in either case, easy prey for his foe.

His feet found a patch of level ground. Instantly he bent his rear leg and went low. Girt's bowie slashed air above his head. Wayne straight-armed his own knife, and Girt had to twist sideways to avoid impaling himself. He backed clear as Wayne straightened.

161

"You're almost good as me, Saddler," Girt said between breaths.

While he was still talking, Wayne lunged, faking high, then cutting low, counting on Girt's own fear for his eyes to distract him. Girt flinched his head away, but he met Wayne's real attack cleanly, his blade blocking it in midstroke. For a space of seconds they stood toe to toe, almost like boxers, cutting and stabbing, bodies weaving like snakes.

Girt ripped upward with a disemboweling stroke, useless except in close quarters like this. Wayne chopped down to meet it. Their hilts locked together, and they strained against one another.

Girt's clawing hand came groping at Wayne's face, as it had during the fight in Heavener. Wayne felt nails claw at him and a finger rake past his lips. He opened his mouth and bit down hard.

Girt howled like he'd taken a hot branding iron on bare flesh. He flung himself backward, shaking his hand furiously. His stubbled face was contorted with rage.

Wayne spat to clear the foulness from his mouth. "Come on, Girt," he taunted. "You ready to try it for real now?"

Girt cursed, waved his outstretched blade back and forth in front of him, then suddenly sprang forward and to the side, coming in on Wayne's right as he had before.

Wayne had been looking for it. He shifted his feet, and brought his bowie up to counter as Girt cut at his arm. The top edge of Wayne's rising blade, with its brass inlay, met Girt's slash. The keen steel of Girt's bowie cut into the softer brass and stuck — exactly as Wayne had intended.

Instantly, before Girt could tug his blade free, Wayne twisted with all the strength of his arm and wrist. Girt's hilt was wrenched half out of his grip before the edge of his knife came free from the brass. He had no way to counter as Wayne thrust between his ribs.

Girt staggered back two paces. His eyes went dull. He fell to his knees.

"Guess it helped me some, after all," Wayne said. He was never sure if Girt heard it before he died.

Wayne threw a long, searching look in the direction of the hollow. There was no sign that their duel had been noticed from Driver's bivouac.

He eyed Girt's body thoughtfully. He hadn't planned on letting Driver know of his visit, but leaving Girt where he lay would only raise questions in Driver's mind when he was discovered, questions that Driver might want answered in blood before he knew the truth of the matter.

Whatever he did, he wasn't likely to be happy about the upshot of it.

Tiredly he trudged back to his horse, not making much of an effort to conceal himself. Driver was going to see him anyway before too much longer.

He wanted to wash his hands after draping Girt's corpse over his saddle. The paint wasn't too happy with the new burden either. Wayne spat again, but the bitterness wouldn't leave his mouth.

Leading the unwilling horse, he started toward

the hollow. As he drew near he saw the figure of a sentry appear among the trees. The fellow stiffened as he caught sight of Wayne.

"Hold it right there!" He was fast enough in bringing his rifle to bear.

Wayne halted, hoping he wasn't running a fool's risk. He was careful not to make any sudden moves. The guard was a young man with the old eyes of a seasoned gunhawk.

"My name's Saddler," Wayne said. "Tell Driver I'm here, and I've got something for him."

"I can see you got something!" the guard snapped. "Step clear of that horse and drop your gun!"

Wayne sighed. No way under heaven he was going in that lion's den unarmed. He raised his voice in a shout. "Hello, the fort!"

The sentry started a little, but then stood firm, eyeing Wayne warily.

"Saddler? Is that you?" Driver's voice rolled out of the hollow.

Wayne glanced at the guard before he answered. "It's me. One of your sentries has me covered. I'm coming in!"

"Jenner?" Driver shouted.

"Yeah, Captain?" The guard didn't take his eyes off Wayne as he answered.

"That the right of it?" Driver's voice called in query.

"Yes, sir! He's got a dead man with him, and he won't give up his guns."

A moment dragged by. Driver was playing it

careful. "Let him keep them!" he shouted. "Saddler, come on in! Resume your post, Jenner!"

"Yes, sir," Jenner called after a grudging moment. He motioned to Wayne with his rifle barrel. "Go on. You heard him."

Wayne kept an eye cocked on him as he led the paint past. Jenner stared at the horse's burden.

"That's Tannery, ain't it?" he asked with an edge of belligerence in his tone.

Wayne came to a halt. "Friend of yours?"

The guard sneered. "Don't reckon he had no friends. But I always figured he'd take a heap of killing."

"He did." Wayne went on toward the hollow. He didn't look back, although he felt the sentry's eyes follow him.

Driver had chosen a good site for his camp, he noted without surprise. The hollow could be defended without becoming a trap for its occupants.

Several hard-bitten men were gathering behind Driver, who stood near a tent that obviously served as his headquarters. Wayne recognized the two gunsels who had backed Driver in the café at Heavener. He recalled Hawken's word that there were eight men riding under Driver's command. Now there was one less, he thought darkly.

Wordlessly he dropped the paint's reins and undid the rope he had used to lash its grisly burden in place. The horse shied nervously, and Girt's body slid unceremoniously from the saddle to sprawl in the dust.

Driver stared down at him with brooding features. "What happened?" he asked tersely as he lifted his head.

"He tried to throw down on me," Wayne told him. "I pulled on him. We settled it with knives. He didn't give me a choice."

Grim interest stirred in Driver's eyes. "You took him with a knife?" he demanded. "How'd you do it?"

"I stabbed him."

Driver snorted. "I think I would've paid to watch." His hand brushed the hilt of his saber.

Wayne didn't bait him further. He was conscious of the pack of hard cases backing Driver. He was on Driver's range here.

"Sorry I had to do in your gold hound."

Driver looked down at the body, his hat brim shielding his eyes. He plucked out a cheroot and fired it. "Forget it," he said without looking up. "Like you said, I don't figure Girt gave you much of a choice. He's been packing a grudge against you ever since the professor hired you on instead of him."

Wayne tried to read something in the predatory faces of Driver's command. He saw only the grudging respect and wary appraisal of fighting men taking stock of one of their own breed. The bitterness lingered in his mouth.

Driver lifted his head and pursed his lips to exhale smoke. "You riding over this way for a reason?" he asked coolly.

Driver was too sharp to be taken in by much of a lie. "I followed you. Figured I owed you a

166

word of thanks for siding with me against those owlhoots."

"You don't owe me a thing," Driver said without a trace of feeling.

With a stabbing motion of his wrist Driver speared the cheroot down at Girt's corpse. It bounced off his chest. Driver gestured about the hollow. "What do you think of my command?" he asked sourly. "It's a far cry from what a man like me should have under him." He pivoted toward the hard cases. "Go on about your duties!" he snapped harshly. "You're dismissed!"

They broke apart without objection or comment.

"Come on, Saddler." Driver strode toward his tent.

Wayne gave it a moment, then followed. Inside the tent Driver had a folding camp table and chair set up next to his cot. Everything was as spartan and orderly as a barracks before inspection.

The only sign of clutter was an open bottle of whiskey and a shot glass on the table. Driver must have been in here drinking alone in the shadows before Wayne's arrival.

Driver lifted the bottle inquiringly.

"I'll pass," Wayne declined.

"Not a drinking man?" Driver poured himself a shot and downed it in one smooth, practiced movement. "You happy as a farmer?" he asked suddenly.

"Happy enough," Wayne allowed. He hesitated, then added, "I figure to get into some ranching as well. I've got my eye on some quarter horse breeding stock and a few head of beef cattle."

Driver shook his head ruefully. "You weren't meant to be a farmer or a rancher any more than I was. You killed two men with your pistol today, and another with your knife, and not a one of them was a tenderfoot. You're a fighting man. It's in your blood."

Wayne recalled the professor's confession that he, too, had viewed him in that same unflattering light. The recollection didn't please him.

"Maybe once," he conceded. "But not any-more."

"I don't buy it." Driver poured, drank again, set the glass down hard enough to almost collapse the table. "How about riding with me? What do you say to you and me as a team? Between us, we could outgun the devil himself!"

Wayne grinned thinly. "It'd never work. Who'd have command?"

Driver threw his head back and laughed. "By thunder, you could be right. Neither one of us would cotton much to taking orders from the other." He sobered quickly. "Still, it's a crying shame the two of us aren't working together."

"I'm a farmer. I'm through fighting other men's fights for a living."

"You work for me, and you'd be fighting your own fights and reaping your own rewards."

Wayne cut his eyes about the tent. Driver's rewards had been sparse so far, he reflected wryly.

"Guess I'll stick to pushing a plow. Maybe run

168

a few head of beeves," he said.

Driver regarded him almost balefully. "If I hadn't seen three men dead by your hand today, I'd say you'd gone soft."

"Those three didn't think so," Wayne said levelly.

Driver let it go by. "Is that the knife you used on Girt?"

"Yep."

"Let's see it." Driver extended a hand.

Reluctantly Wayne passed it to him. Driver tested the point and edge, then ran a thumbnail through the new nick in the brass.

"This how you did it?" he inquired. "You let his blade wedge here?"

"He did it himself," Wayne said.

Driver hefted the knife thoughtfully. "I haven't seen a blade rigged like this in a long time. Most of them are made in factories these days. You had this one made personal. It takes a man who really knows cold steel to make that trick work." He reversed the bowie handily and returned it, hilt first. "You ever crossed sabers with another man?" His eyes glinted.

"Never for real," Wayne lied. His experiences with a sword were none of Driver's business.

He remembered the fencing tournaments that had been part of the recreation of every post where he'd served. Unless the opponents were settling something in private, the blades had always been padded to avoid serious injury.

"I went up for real against a tinhorn lieutenant

169

back in the cavalry," Driver recounted as if relishing the memory. "It was over a woman. The lieutenant thought he was something fancy with a blade. I showed him otherwise. I couldn't kill him because that would've meant a court-martial. But he'll carry some scars to his grave. The fool woman up and married him after that. Wouldn't give me the time of day. I'm telling you, Saddler, there's no justice for free-living men like us, except what we make ourselves!"

"I better be riding," Wayne said.

Driver came back from his reminiscing. "Suit yourself. Obliged to you for letting me know about Girt."

Wayne paused at the tent mouth. "You planning on staying up here to look for his strike?"

Driver chewed it over like the butt of one of his cheroots. "I'll have to give that some thought."

Wayne kept his face expressionless. He had been hoping that Driver and his pack would ride down off the mountain now that their guide was dead.

"Be seeing you." He stepped out of the tent before Driver could snap him a salute.

Girt's body still lay limply where it had fallen. Driver needed to order a burial detail. Wayne felt the gunslicks gauging him as he walked to the paint and mounted. He didn't like putting his back to them when he rode out. There was no sign of the guard Jenner.

Wayne checked his backtrail every so often as he rode. He wouldn't put it past Driver to deploy a man to keep an eye on him.

Finally, from the edge of a backward glance he caught the tail end of a movement that might have been a mounted figure passing through the trees. Wayne reined the paint upslope over bare rocks and guided him in among a stand of saplings where he commanded a good view. Unlimbering his Winchester, he laid it across his saddle and waited.

After a time he heard the rustle of hooves in the carpet of leaves. He lifted the Winchester. In a moment a hawkfaced gunman rode into view below him. The jasper drew up and cast about with a puzzled look on his face. Likely he'd been tracking by sign as well as sight, and now he'd lost both. He wasn't toting a rifle, which meant he put a powerful lot of stock in his handiness with a six-gun.

"Dogging a man's trail can get you killed," Wayne said from among the saplings.

The gunslick froze in his saddle. Then, very casually, he moved, turning only his head to gaze up at the small grove of saplings. This was a cool one, Wayne thought.

"Just following orders," he drawled as his eyes picked out Wayne's form among the small trees. Wayne was sure he didn't miss the rifle. "Driver said to see where you were headed. If I was stalking you with a mind to put a bullet through your head, you'd never know it."

Cool *and* hard, Wayne acknowledged silently. "You're the one under the gun," he pointed out. "You can tell Driver he knows where I'm headed."

Wayne paused a beat. "Tell him thanks for his offer — and to say a few words over Girt's grave for me."

Hawkface smirked. "I'll tell him."

Wayne didn't like his smirk. The notion of this gun artist skulking around the camp while Laura was there didn't sit well with him.

"Keep following me, and I'll kill you," he said deliberately.

The smirk vanished. "You'd better bring help if you try."

Wayne shifted the Winchester until it was lined on his chest. "From where I'm sitting, I don't need any."

Looking into the barrel of a rifle, Hawkface had enough sense not to buck the odds. Expertly he backed his horse from in front of the grove. With a last glare flung in Wayne's direction, he put his horse about and headed back toward Driver's base.

Wayne watched long enough to be sure he wasn't going to turn around. The sooner Driver and all his sorry cohorts cleared out, the happier he'd be.

He rode a meandering route back to the camp, keeping an eye peeled for Hawkface or anyone else. He wasn't followed. Hopefully, Driver would be satisfied with his underling's report.

As he rode into camp he saw Hastings kneeling almost reverently in front of the smaller rune stone. The professor was gazing raptly up past the rocky wall of the ravine. He looked sharply about at the sound of Wayne's horse but made no effort to rise or greet him. He studied the runes and other carvings for a moment, then once more turned his gaze up the mountain.

Laura reached Wayne by the time he dismounted. Her eyes widened at the grim set of his face and the slump of his shoulders.

"What happened?" she asked.

Wayne hesitated, but figured he may as well tell her. "Girt Tannery jumped me. I had to kill him."

She gasped and the blood drained from her face. "Did he hurt you?"

Wayne shook his head. "Never touched me."

He felt an aching desire to hold her and be comforted by her arms.

"Let me take your horse," she said. Her hand brushed against his as she all but snatched the reins from him and hurried away.

Wayne shook his head wearily and looked about for a shovel. He still had bodies to bury.

CHAPTER 14

"We're pulling out," Nolen Driver announced to Wayne and the Hastingses. "My men have had enough of this mountain. I gave the order to break camp this morning. Thought I'd ride over and say my good-byes."

He sat his big Appaloosa easily, just within the box canyon. The spirited animal shifted and side-stepped beneath him. Wayne tried to read the feelings behind Driver's facial expression and arrogant manner.

"So, you're giving up prospecting?" Wayne asked.

Driver shrugged. "I never did put much stock in it paying off," he confessed. "And with Girt dead, there's no point in fooling around with it any further. No hard feelings, incidentally, for you having put a blade in him."

Beside him, Wayne sensed Laura's shudder. He hadn't given her the details of his knife duel with Girt the day before. The professor was standing nearby and did not register much reaction.

Watching Driver, Wayne thought the big ex-cavalryman didn't look like a man whose plans had suffered a major defeat. Rather, he was like the spirited horse he rode, chomping at the bit and ready to go into action.

"Miss Hastings, I regret that I won't get another chance to sample your fine cooking."

Laura smiled wanly.

"Professor, the best of luck with your treasure hunting." Driver smiled cold-bloodedly.

"The only treasure I seek is knowledge," Hastings answered stiffly.

"Saddler, maybe our paths will cross again," Driver turned his attention at last to Wayne.

"Lord willing," Wayne responded.

Driver sneered. "Yeah, Lord willing. By the way, my man gave me your message." He snapped a final salute and wheeled the Appaloosa about.

They watched him depart. Laura was standing so close to Wayne that he was sorely tempted to encircle her shoulders with his arm. He restrained the urge. Her father was present, and even if he hadn't been, there was no way to tell how Laura would react to such an overt gesture of affection.

Driver's duster faded from view among the trees. Laura glanced up at Wayne. He expected her to speak, but she remained silent. What did she want of him, for pete's sake? he wondered with a disturbing twinge of irritation. He had all but declared his love for her, and here she was, treating him like he was some kind of outcast.

Her father cleared his throat. "Now that we have the mountain to ourselves, so to speak, do you have any objection to my making certain forays on my own?"

Wayne pulled his mind off Laura and her unpredictable moods. "Just as soon as I'm sure they're gone," he answered. "But don't go too far astray."

He waited until noon before saddling the paint and setting out for the site of Driver's encampment. He took his time, staying to cover where possible and keeping his eyes peeled. He spotted a deer and glimpsed the rugged shapes of a pack of razorback hogs among the trees. But he didn't see any sign of human life.

He also noted that there had been no trace of the reclusive Hawken since his single visit to the camp. Wayne speculated that he still could be lurking about. Or had that brief contact with humanity been enough to send him retreating back into the remote seclusion of his mountain? A vague sense of sadness touched Wayne at the thought.

He approached the hollow cautiously, but the lack of woodsmoke and human voices told him before he ever laid eyes on it that the bivouac was deserted.

Driver had done a thorough job of breaking camp, he saw as he guided the paint into the hollow. As if commanding a cavalry patrol in hostile territory, he had had his men clear virtually all traces of their stay. It was a far cry from the many despoiled sites of even brief human habitation Wayne had seen in his time. If not for his tendencies toward violence, Driver might once have had the makings of a better than fair officer, he admitted with some reluctance.

The prints leaving the hollow were easy to follow. Driver's command hadn't been gone long. Taking it easy, Wayne stayed with the tracks until they emerged on a trail of sorts that snaked its way down the mountain.

From a rocky promontory, he spotted the band of horsemen just coming out on the flatlands far below. Even from this distance Driver's white-coated figure was plainly visible. Driver had his men riding four abreast, in the approved riding order of a mounted force, even though they were one man short of two lines. Driver led ahead of them.

Wayne watched until the tiny squad had vanished in the haze of the grasslands. That was it, then, he thought. As Hastings had said, now they had the mountain to themselves.

Professor Trevor Hastings balanced precariously atop the rocky outcropping he had scaled, and strained to match the contours of the slope with the memorized markings on the sheet carefully folded in his pocket.

It wasn't easy. How much would the topography of the mountain have changed over the centuries? How many landmarks and geographical features would have been eroded away by the relentless abrasions of wind and rain? Some of them, certainly, but not all. The brooding presence of the giant rune stone, standing in splendid majesty, was evidence that not everything had changed since the days when the Viking Glome had trod this land as his own.

Of late, Hastings had found himself feeling a strange kinship with the long-dead adventurer and explorer, as though Glome's spirit might actually be reaching out a spectral hand to draw him on. Pagan nonsense, he knew, but the eerie perception lingered nonetheless.

He had left the camp in the early light of morning and made his way on foot up the mountain.

"I shall be surveying the slope above our camp," he had explained patiently in response to Wayne's query. "It is not necessary for you to accompany me."

"Don't wander too far," Wayne cautioned.

"I'm well armed," Hastings had reminded him, touching the flap of the holster on his belt. "You've no need to worry."

Wayne shrugged. "Sing out if you run into trouble," he advised. "I'll come looking if you're not back by noon."

"Very well," Hastings agreed.

Laura had seemed nervous about his departure. Hastings was surprised that the tension between her and Wayne had actually increased since he had given Laura his blessings to accept Wayne as a beau.

Ascending the slope had been difficult in spots, and he found a sturdy branch to use as a walking stick. Avoiding the sheer walls that loomed in places and pausing frequently to consult his notes, he had worked his way upward.

Now, balanced atop the outcropping, he grinned in satisfaction as his eyes took in the contours of the grade above him. Half sliding, he scrambled from his perch and dusted himself off.

A shaft of sunlight, filtering through the trees from overhead, made him blink. What time was it? he wondered abruptly. In his absorption with his project, he had let the hours slip by almost unheeded. He checked his pocket watch. He would start back soon, but it wouldn't hurt to proceed a bit farther, particularly when he had come so close to his goal. The decision made, he looked about for the walking stick he had discarded in order to scale the boulders.

"How's treasure hunting, Professor?" someone said from the woods to his left.

Hastings turned sharply. Shock surged in him as he made out a good half-dozen horsemen lurking in the shadows. He had been completely unaware of their approach.

Automatically he reached for the pistol holstered at his waist.

"I wouldn't, Professor," Nolen Driver said firmly.

Hastings became aware that several of the riders had rifles or six-guns trained on him. Slowly he moved his hand away from his holster.

"Wise decision." Driver moved his big mount forward and grinned around the cheroot clamped firmly between his teeth. "I think it's time you and I had a talk, Professor."

"I wonder where Dad could be," Laura remarked. "Lunch is almost ready."

Wayne glanced up at the sky. It was nigh onto noon. He frowned.

"What's wrong?" Laura asked quickly.

"I told him to be back by about now."

"There's probably no need to worry. Sometimes he gets so absorbed in his work that he loses track of time."

"I've noticed."

She smiled, and he felt his spirits lift.

They had spoken little during the long hours of the morning. Wayne had busied himself with camp chores and tending to the horses. He'd neglected those tasks some during the past couple of days, what with prowling the mountain to try to keep track of Driver and his cohorts. Laura had spent the morning organizing and editing her father's scribbled notes on the excavations in the canyon.

"I'll finish lunch. Surely he'll be back by the time I'm done."

Laura and Wayne talked about one thing or another as she worked. She was showing more warmth and friendliness than she had in some time. Wayne noted that she appeared most at ease with him when she had some job or duty with which to occupy herself.

He listened to her with half an ear. He knew he ought to be enjoying this time with her, but a nagging worm of uneasiness was beginning to gnaw at him. He should have gone with Hastings. . . .

"It's ready." Laura's smile faded as she saw

Wayne's face. "You're worried about him, aren't you?" she asked intently.

He nodded. "I may be fretting over nothing, but he's been gone long enough. I better go take a look for him."

"I'm coming with you," she said immediately.

If Hastings had gotten into a bind, Wayne didn't like the idea of dragging her along with him to search. But the notion of leaving her alone here in camp didn't sit well either.

"Okay," he consented. "But you do what I tell you if trouble comes up. And be sure to take your guns. Get your father's big-game rifle, too."

Her eyes grew wide and still. "Do you really think something has happened to him?"

"I hope not," Wayne said, putting her off. He wasn't sure what to think, but he didn't like the sense of apprehension he was feeling. "Let's get the horses. We'll take your dad's along. He was on foot."

She set about packing the lunch for later. Mounted, they rode out of the canyon. Wayne had no trouble striking the professor's trail above the ravine. He squinted down at it as he rode, raising his head occasionally to check their surroundings.

"Keep your eyes peeled for company," he said tersely.

"I may as well," Laura returned, "because, for the life of me, I can't see what in the world it is that you're following."

"He was using a walking stick. Its impressions are easy to pick out. Other than some pauses

181

and sidetracking, he seems to have known where he was going." Wayne paused, then turned to her and asked, "Any idea what he was looking for?"

"None. He's been a little secretive of late, but he often gets that way on a dig. I assumed he was just going on a general survey today. I can't imagine what destination he might've had in mind."

Time dragged past them. Then a rugged pile of boulders loomed ahead. Wayne saw where the tracks led to it. In several places the lichen had been abraded from the surface of the rock. Hastings had clambered atop the pile for a better view, he surmised.

Wayne pulled up, studying the formation. Then the hairs at the back of his neck bristled. Leaning against the base of the outcropping, exactly as it might have been placed by a hiker preparing to climb the rocks, was a sturdy branch. It showed fresh marks where smaller twigs had been broken off to allow for a hand to grip it more easily. Dirt covered the end resting on the ground.

"There's his walking stick," he said bleakly.

He heard Laura's gasp. He dismounted and went over to pick up the branch. He started to call out, then reined in the impulse. Dropping the stick, he moved away from the rocks.

The prints of the horses' hooves were easy to find. The riders had apparently been rounding the mountain, coming upslope, hence his own failure to cross their trail earlier. His eyes fell on something amid the thin carpet of leaves. Going to one knee, he picked it up.

"What is it?" Laura asked, coming up behind him.

She broke off with a little exclamation as she recognized the butt of the half-smoked cheroot he held between thumb and forefinger.

"Driver," Wayne said through his teeth. "He and his men have your father."

"What do you mean?" Laura cried.

Wayne uncoiled to his feet. He flung the cheroot sharply aside. "He foxed me," he said almost to himself. "Leaving the mountain was just a ruse so I'd figure they were gone. Once they were clear, they circled around and came up from the backside. They were probably headed for our camp when they stumbled on your dad." Bitterness edged his tone. "Shoot, the whole business of them coming up here to look for gold must've just been a ploy so they could eventually get their hands on him!"

"But why would they want him?" Anguish and confusion showed on her face.

"I should've tumbled to it before now," Wayne said, berating himself. "Driver was talking all the time about us looking for treasure. I think he figures your father knows where there's a cache of Viking gold or some such thing. He got tired of waiting on us to lead him to it and decided to take matters into his own hands."

"But there isn't any gold!"

"Driver will take a heap of convincing to swallow that."

"We've got to try to get Dad away from them!"

"Yeah," Wayne agreed grimly. "We do."

CHAPTER 15

"I am not an ignorant man, Professor," Nolen Driver boasted. "I may not have Captain Saddler's West Point education to my credit, but I have read widely and taught myself many things." He broke off with a hard laugh. "And parts of my education go way beyond any book learning!"

Hastings didn't doubt it for a minute. From where he sat with his back against rough stone, his hands bound behind him, he gazed flatly at his captor and tried not to let fear show in his eyes.

"As I've already told you, you're wasting your time, Captain Driver." Hastings was gratified his voice held steady. Humoring the man and his pretensions was galling, but it seemed to be the best course. Heaven knew, there was little else he could do at the moment.

He cast his eyes about his prison and saw nothing to encourage him. Cut by running water flowing past the base of a low ridge, the rocky niche might be a cave in another million years, if the surrounding strata didn't collapse. Located atop a mesalike formation of the mountain, it made an ideal hideout for Driver and his pack of cutthroats.

Hastings could see none of the other hard cases

at present, but he knew they were near the overhang because snatches of their coarse voices reached him occasionally. Even if he could get past their leader — a virtual impossibility to begin with — there would be no way to evade them and get off the mesa.

Freedom seemed very distant.

"I've studied the Vikings, Professor," Driver was continuing as he strode animatedly about, ducking his head at times to avoid the low ceiling. The scabbard of his saber banged against his leg as he paced.

"They were raiders — pirates and barbarians who looted and pillaged everywhere they struck. The wealth they accumulated over the centuries must've been enormous!" Driver's eyes gleamed avariciously in the dim light.

"Most of the so-called wealth they accumulated consisted of perishable items, long since consumed or decayed," Hastings said, repeating the same argument he had employed — futilely, it appeared — back in their camp. "Further, all items that might be termed treasure were gradually lost in one way or another — barter, trade, conquest — as the Viking culture dissolved. Some rare artifacts have been unearthed by archaeologists or discovered by collectors, but there was never any central storehouse of Viking gold — certainly not here on the North American continent!"

"But some of them reached here," Driver shot back, obviously unswayed by the lecture on Viking history and culture. "That rune stone proves they were here, doesn't it? You told me so yourself."

"True," Hastings conceded. "A small band apparently did dwell in this region centuries ago. But there is no evidence of any treasure."

His scholar's soul compelled him to try to dissuade Driver, although he knew his efforts were probably useless. But so long as he kept the outlaw chieftain talking, Driver was unlikely to move on to several other possible choices of action that had occurred to Hastings. None of them were appealing.

"I don't buy it." Driver stopped his pacing and fixed Hastings with those glittering eyes.

"I assure you, sir, I am not lying," Hastings asserted with as much dignity as he could muster.

"Don't give me that, Professor." Driver shook his head slowly back and forth. "You wouldn't have come all the way out here to the Territory, and stayed up on this mountain poking around for as long as you have, if there wasn't something more to find than an old rock with a few carvings on it."

"I've only been here a matter of days," Hastings protested, with genuine consternation at the man's ignorance. "It would take months, even years, to do a proper study of the rune stone and survey this mountain for artifacts!"

Driver ignored him. He resumed his spirited pacing. "When Tannery came to me with his scheme of hiring on as your guide so he could lead you up the mountain where we'd be waiting to do a little pillaging of our own, I saw right

187

away he was setting his sights too low. I knew if we waited and let you have your head, you'd eventually lead us right to the treasure. Then Girt had to go and get himself fired, which messed up everything. So, I cooked up the idea of making like we were looking for gold so we could keep an eye on you."

"You should've merely waited and been patient, then you would have seen that there was no treasure," Hastings said stiffly.

"I was fed up with waiting, and so were my men. Besides, Saddler was nosing around too much. He was starting to get his back up. When he killed Girt, I figured we needed to act. Without Girt, I didn't have anybody who knew his way around the mountain. We made like we were leaving so as to pull the wool over Saddler's eyes. I knew he'd be watching. Then we circled around and came back up on the other side. I deployed my men above your camp with the plan of launching an attack." Driver turned a cold smile on him. "But you saved us the trouble by walking right into our arms."

"If you expect me to lead to some cache of Viking gold, you're wasting your time!"

"Don't wager too much on that," Driver advised. "I can be mighty persuasive when I need to be."

Hastings felt icy sweat on his forehead. "If there was any gold," he said as emphatically as he could, "I would lead you to it. The plain fact is that you are chasing a phantom, a will-of-the-wisp. The treasure exists only in your imagination."

"I know better, Professor. If a clan of Vikings came to this continent to settle, then it only stands to reason they would bring their wealth with them."

Hastings ground his teeth in frustration. Driver's obsessive lust for wealth made rational discourse impossible.

"Even here in the Territory there are laws," Hastings tried a new tack. "You won't be permitted to get away with this."

"Laws?" Driver echoed scornfully. He gave a burst of laughter that bounced harshly from the stone walls and ceiling. "On this mountain I'm the law! If Saddler comes after you, I've made plans to stop him. Even if he does get this far, he can't fight all of us!"

He stalked closer to Hastings until he stood towering over him, hands on his hips. The thin veneer of culture again sloughed away like the skin of a snake.

"This is the way of it, Professor. You ain't got any choice but to deal with me. You savvy that?"

Hastings forced his eyes to drop. "I need some time," he said softly, in the only remaining ploy he could think of. "You have to let me consider this."

"Now you're being reasonable." Driver drew back. "Sure, I'll give you a few minutes to chew it over."

He turned and made as if to stride out from under the overhang. He took two steps, then, with no warning, he pivoted on the balls of his feet, the saber rasping free from its sheath as he turned. All as part of the same surge of motion, he executed a flawless fencing lunge, forward knee bent, rear leg outstretched. The tip of his blade, vibrating only the tiniest bit, halted no more than an inch from the throat of his prisoner.

For a heartbeat Driver held the stance. "Just don't take too long to make up your mind," he whispered down the length of arm and blade.

Hastings pulled his eyes away from the deadly point hovering so close to his life's blood. He couldn't nod; he could barely even swallow.

"I understand," he managed to stammer.

Driver laughed and straightened. He slid his sword back into its scabbard without breaking his gaze into his prisoner's face. "I'll hold you to that, Professor."

He smiled with as much warmth as the steel of the saber, then swung about on his heel so sharply that the tail of his duster snapped behind him. Without looking back, he marched out into the afternoon sunlight.

Hastings tried to regain his composure. As his heartbeat slowed to normal, he became aware of the hard stone gouging uncomfortably into his back and the ropes cutting painfully into his wrists. He did his best to ignore such physical discomforts. Instead, he focused his mind on the problem before him.

He was a scientist and a scholar, a disciplined thinker. Surely he could outwit Driver. But Hastings had never been in greater danger in all the adventuresome years spent excavating remote archaeological sites around the globe.

He did not dare count on Wayne to somehow rescue him. Granted that Wayne was an experienced fighting man, he would be pitted against tremendous odds, assuming he could find this hiding place.

Any hope of Wayne's finding him was also tempered by fear that Laura would insist on being a part of any rescue effort. Hastings shuddered.

Resolutely he walled his fears into a back part of his mind. Whatever time he had would best be spent in trying to formulate a strategy.

Driver would never be convinced there was no lost Viking treasure. But if he could be persuaded that his prisoner was willing, albeit grudgingly, to lead him to a cache of gold, he might relax his guard, particularly if he were convinced that his captive was weak and helpless. Deluding the cynical ex-soldier wouldn't be easy, Hastings knew. Driver would be suspicious of a quick capitulation from him. To convince his captor, he would probably have to undergo some form of physical persuasion. At least that would give him an excuse to appear injured, he concluded darkly.

The ropes seemed tighter than ever. He shifted uselessly to gain some relief. He had done all that was within his own ability. Now the future was up to a power beyond him. He couldn't clasp his numb hands, but he bowed his head nonetheless and prayed for succor.

"Wayne, I've been thinking," Laura said in a strained voice, riding behind him on the trail. "Maybe we should go back to Heavener and try to find Heck Thomas. He could get help."

Wayne shook his head. "Heck's long gone. And even if he was there, by the time we got a posse together and came all the way back, it would likely be too late for your father. While we were looking for help, Driver would be doing his best to get your dad to tell him where the gold is. He's not going to be easy to convince that there isn't any lost treasure." He twisted about in the saddle to study her with concern. "How are you holding up?"

She smiled weakly. Her face was drawn tight with strain. "I'm fine."

Wayne was having second thoughts about bringing her along. But he still couldn't see much in the way of alternatives. He gave her a nod that he hoped was reassuring, and faced front again.

The tracks had led them steadily upward, and the outlaws had made no effort to conceal the trail. Not for the first time, Wayne wondered how Driver's mind was working. He would surely be expecting Wayne to be after him, and it was good military procedure to mount a rear guard. Which meant, Wayne concluded, that somewhere up ahead he and Laura were liable to ride into a bushwhacker's sights if they weren't careful.

Wayne hauled up on the reins, and the paint halted abruptly. He heard the click of hooves as

Laura reined in behind him.

"What is it?" she asked.

Wayne used his chin to point. "I don't like the looks of that rift up yonder."

From the edge of the trees where they had halted, the slope climbed to a wide gap that an ancient cataclysm had split in a massive bulge of the mountain. Rocky walls lined either side of the pass. The ruggedness of the grade made it out of the question to bypass the gap. A sharpshooter perched on one of the cliffs would have a dandy shot at any target moving along the draw.

"Do you think they're waiting for us there?" Laura queried.

"I think somebody is."

Methodically he scanned the rims of the cliffs bordering the pass. He hoped the afternoon sunlight might glint off carelessly exposed metal, betraying a bushwhacker's position. But he saw only the dark, brooding faces of the opposing walls. Either whoever waited was too good to give himself away, or Wayne was mistaken about there being anyone there at all.

He didn't figure he was mistaken.

They had not yet emerged from the trees into the open area fronting the pass, so it was a safe bet they hadn't yet been spotted. Wayne scowled thoughtfully. They didn't have time for this sort of stalking game, but only a tenderfoot would ride openly into a suspected ambush.

"What are you thinking?" Laura asked.

"Let me have your dad's hunting rifle."

He reached back and felt the cold metal weight of the big double-bore gun fill his hand as she passed it to him.

"It's loaded," she advised.

Wayne dismounted and slid his Winchester from the saddle sheath. He hefted one rifle in each hand and cocked his head to look up at Laura.

"Give me about twenty minutes, then spook your dad's horse so he'll head through that gap, the faster the better. Don't show yourself."

She nodded. "Where are you going to be?"

"I'm going to circle through these trees and get up along that rim there. I'm hoping I'll spot the bushwhacker, or that he'll give himself away when the horse goes past. Maybe I can get a shot at him then."

She looked doubtful.

"Twenty minutes," he repeated, and slipped away among the trees.

He kept to the cover of the woods, catfooting as swiftly as he dared. Carrying both rifles hindered him, but the heavy caliber of the Rigby might give him an edge in firepower.

The wooded area extended almost even with the base of the great hump that was split in two by the pass. For a moment Wayne crouched at the edge of the trees and tried to pick out the best route to the top. He still had seen no sign of any drygulcher. All he had to go on was his knowledge of Driver's nature and the first faint pricklings at the nape of his neck.

Gathering himself, he eased from cover and

darted across twenty yards of open stone to the shelter of a rugged boulder at the hill's base. Peering upward, he evaluated what lay ahead of him. In addition to watching his step on the treacherous patches of loose stone, he was going to have to keep an eye out for the bushwhacker.

He shoved the smaller Winchester butt first down the back of his shirt. It was devilishly uncomfortable; the rifle had a tendency to shift about and gouge him in a new spot at every step. But it left one of his hands free.

Silently he worked his way up through the rocks. How much time had passed? he wondered. Halfway up he stopped to reconnoiter. The sun glared down on him, and he had to fight the urge to snatch the irritating Winchester from his back.

From his position he seemed to have a good view all along the fifty-yard rim above him. He couldn't find any sign of a waiting marksman. Maybe the hombre was on the other side of the draw.

He crept onward, eyes searching the rocks, ears pricked for sounds, nostrils testing the air for scents. The faint rustle of scales on stone made him turn his head sharply. He caught just a glimpse of what could have been the huge red-and-brown-banded body of a poisonous copperhead vanishing into the blackness of a rocky niche. He didn't think any copperhead grew to be that big.

He steered clear of the niche and clambered the last dozen feet to the rim. Warily he lifted his head. Fifty feet below him was the bare floor of the pass. Runoff from higher up the mountain had kept it scoured clear of debris and dirt, so no vegetation had taken root there.

The opposite wall was thirty yards away. He squinted against the heat waves and ran his eyes along its rim. Still, he detected nothing.

Gratefully he eased the Winchester from its uncomfortable riding place. He laid it gently on the rock beside him and shifted the Rigby so it was close at hand, careful to keep the barrels of both weapons in the shade. He was too good to let himself be given away by a betraying gleam.

He had never fired the big Rigby, but its heavy .416 caliber, he knew, was capable of dropping even the largest big-game animal in its tracks if the hunter's aim was good. It might also be used to flush an unsuspecting target from cover.

Kneeling in the shelter of a low stone ridge, he tested the feel of the Rigby against his shoulder, just as the clatter of hooves on stone sounded from down the pass. He didn't know what Laura had done to spook the horse, but the animal came tearing into sight at a run. Wayne snapped his eyes away from it, and scanned the opposite cliff wall. He doubted Driver's man could be startled into letting off a shot at a riderless horse, but he might make the mistake of showing himself, however briefly.

A twitch of motion on the far rim caught Wayne's eye. It was a man's shoulder, briefly exposed as its owner tried to get a better look at the fleeing horse.

Wayne didn't hesitate. He lined the Rigby on the pile of boulders where he'd seen the movement and touched off both bores at once. The butt slammed against his shoulder as if it were a battering ram. The twin blast was like a cannon going off. Stone and rock dust exploded from the boulders. A figure reared into view, pawing at his blinded eyes. Wayne set the Rigby aside, snatched up the Winchester, and fired from the shoulder, all in one smooth burst of movement. The drygulcher jerked, then rocked forward. Wayne fired again, and his target plunged headfirst to the floor of the pass.

Wayne ducked and looked hastily about, but no other enemies showed themselves, and no more shots sounded. Reassured that the bushwhacker had been by himself, he gazed down at the sprawled figure until he was sure it wouldn't move again.

Sometimes killing was a job that needed to be done, he reminded himself grimly. Laura would be worried; he should be getting back to her. Then they needed to round up the professor's horse and get on the scent again.

Picking up the Rigby, he straightened to his feet. He paused long enough to stare at what he could see of the face of the mountain still looming above him. Driver and his sordid command were up there somewhere. They would have heard the gunshots, and Driver might guess that his man wasn't going to be back. He would be waiting for them to come.

CHAPTER 16

"Do you think that's where they have him?" Laura whispered close at Wayne's side.

"I'd bet on it," he answered.

She peered past him, craning her neck to gaze up at the odd formation where Wayne had caught a glimmer of light in the gathering dusk.

Even without that telltale sign and the tracks they had followed, he might have guessed that the formation was where Nolen Driver would make his stand. A jagged out-thrust from the side of the mountain had weathered into a sort of miniature mesa. The runoff had undercut a high stone ridge at its rear, creating a shallow cave.

Wayne had yet to make out any human forms, but he knew they were lurking up there. He could see only one route to the summit. Sheer walls made up the other sides of the mesa. He was unable to see beyond the ridge that housed the shallow cave, but he suspected there would be a sheer drop there as well.

Driver must have selected this site ahead of time, and Wayne had to give the ex-soldier credit. From such a vantage point, he and his men could hold off a small army, much less a former soldier and an inexperienced young woman bent on snatching a captive from their midst.

With the Rigby reloaded and the professor's horse once again on a lead rope, they had left the bushwhacker where he lay, and pressed after their quarry. Wayne kept a watchful eye on Laura, noting that stress and fatigue were beginning to wear her down. He had insisted she eat some jerky while they took a brief rest in the late afternoon. Fretfully, she had done so, but her furrowed brow and lackluster eyes told him she was riding a ragged edge.

Now, with their prey cornered, she seemed to have been granted a new strength. Her eyes had lost their dullness, and her mouth was set determinedly.

"What do we do?" she asked without taking her gaze from the cave.

Wayne cast a look upward. The summit was still above them. Driver had chosen his site well enough, but unless a bivouac was at the very top of a mountain, someone could always command the higher ground. One man with a rifle, stationed a little farther up the peak, might be able to keep Driver and his cohorts pinned down for a vital few minutes.

One man, he thought, or one woman.

"You can give me some cover from up yonder." He pointed as he replied to her question.

"What are you planning?" She turned wide eyes on him.

"I'm going in there after your dad."

This had gone on long enough, Professor Trevor Hastings decided firmly. He had suffered sufficient physical punishment at the sadistic hands of the big outlaw known as Bull so that his capitulation would be quite believable. But, while his body ached abominably, and his skull throbbed like it was near to splitting open, he was not seriously injured. For the next stage of his dubious plan, he needed to convince Driver that the exact opposite was true.

Gingerly he shifted his position where they had left him propped against the wall of the stone overhang. He had been allowed water but no food. Outside, he could see darkness growing. He got as comfortable as he could, and waited for the sounds in the camp to die down. Driver had given him until morning to reconsider his refusal to cooperate.

He could see the shape of his guard silhouetted against the mouth of his stone prison. It was the young outlaw, Jenner. As the banked fire died down, his figure grew dim. Hastings thought he heard Driver's voice, and repressed an involuntary shudder at the notion of the ringleader's return, possibly accompanied by the burly Bull.

At last, when the voices were silent, Hastings rolled awkwardly onto his back. He arched his spine and drummed his heels against the stone floor.

"Help!" he gasped, letting the word trail off into a gurgle.

"Huh?" Jenner turned quickly in his direction.

Hastings repeated his performance, adding some writhing for good measure. His contortions were agonizing to his bruised body. It didn't take much acting to collapse limply and pant for air when he was finished.

"What's ailing you?" Jenner's form loomed over him, a shielded lantern uplifted. He peered anxiously down.

"Can't breathe!" Hastings choked. "Chest's on fire! My heart!"

Jenner backed away with a stifled oath. He set the lantern down and hurried outside.

"Captain!" Hastings heard him call. "You better come quick, and bring Doc!"

Voices muttered and cursed. Hastings twisted his upper body back and forth and groaned.

Driver's face, demonic in the dim light of the lantern, gazed fiercely down at him. "What are you pulling, Professor?" he snarled.

Hastings gurgled, sucked for air, drummed his heels. "Heart!" he cried weakly. "Burning . . ." He trailed off into a moan.

Another figure joined Driver. "Take a look, Doc!" Driver commanded. "He says it's his heart!"

"I keep telling you, I worked for a horse vet for a while," Doc grumbled. "That don't make me no blamed people doctor!" His broad, unshaven face wore an expression of displeasure.

But he dropped to his knees and felt his patient's forehead with a surprisingly gentle hand. Then he pressed his palm to the professor's chest. Hastings could feel his own heart pounding from his exertions.

"Heart's going wild," Doc confirmed. "Get the ropes off him so I can check him better!"

Driver's saber gleamed in the lantern light. Hastings felt the touch of cold steel, then the blessed relief of the bonds falling from his wrists. He flung his body into a new spasm that had Doc spitting oaths as he tried to hold him down.

Hastings went limp, stuck his tongue out, and let his eyes roll back in his head. He had no medical training himself, but he doubted Doc's shaky skills qualified him to diagnose a heart attack, or anything else for that matter.

"I'll get some water," Driver offered. He turned and strode outside, ordering his followers clear of the mouth of the overhang as he did so. He had sounded a little rattled, Hastings was pleased to note.

Doc probed and prodded. Hastings lay limply. It dawned on him that his ploy was working far better than he could have anticipated. He had not bargained on having his hands freed. His arms were sore, but the ropes hadn't been tight enough to cut off all circulation, so he guessed he would still have partial use of his hands.

He realized he might never have a better chance than this. If he could get outside, the darkness would give him cover. Driver's men were groggy and confused after being roused from sleep, and none of them were under the overhang except the one called Doc.

With no warning, Hastings went into another fit, flailing and gasping. Doc recoiled with a curse. Hastings swiveled his body about. He yanked both knees to his chest and then kicked both feet out, as he had once had occasion to see a sturdy Frenchman do in a brawl. The heels of his boots collided with Doc's face and flung him sprawling backward.

Hastings scrambled on top of him, fumbling with clumsy fingers for the pistol at his belt. Doc was too stunned to resist. Hastings felt his hand close awkwardly on the pistol. He pulled it clear. He had to use both thumbs to ear back the hammer.

He lurched to his feet. None of his limbs wanted to work right, but he was up and moving, and he was no longer helpless.

Then a familiar scabbard-slung figure materialized before him. Hastings pulled up short. A canteen was in Driver's right hand, or Hastings felt sure the outlaw would have pulled his sidearm by sheer reflex.

"Let me by," Hastings warned. His voice was a rasping croak.

Driver didn't move. He bared his teeth in an expression that might have been a smile, or a snarl, or maybe both, in the poor light. "So, you were funning me, Professor. That was a pretty good act, but this is as far as it goes."

"This is no act." Hastings grunted hoarsely and jabbed the barrel of the gun forward.

The stone walls seemed to spin around him. His

legs were wobbly. He tried to hold the six-gun steady on Driver's ominous shape. Awareness grew in him that he would have to shoot Driver, should have shot him immediately instead of hesitating. It wouldn't be murder, not under these circumstances.

"Put the gun down, Professor," Driver advised coldly. "You'll never make it off the mesa."

"What in thunder?" a coarse voice exclaimed.

Involuntarily Hastings swung his head toward the sound. He glimpsed the familiar bulky shape of Bull just outside the overhang, even as he understood that it had been a terrible mistake to take his eyes off Driver.

The whisper of the blade being pulled from its scabbard warned him. But before he could turn his gaze back to Driver, the edge of the cavalry saber crashed down on the six-gun, wrenching it from his weakened fingers. In the next second the same keen edge slashed across to halt resting against his throat.

Hastings held himself very still.

"Don't tempt me beyond my means, Professor," Driver said through gritted teeth. "I don't like being tricked, and I won't let it happen again. I've dreamed all my life about a chance like this. I need you alive, but you have to learn you can't cross me without paying dearly. So far, I've had Bull go easy on you, but no more. You hear me? No more!"

"I'll take you to the gold," Hastings whispered past the steel kissing his throat.

For a moment Driver's eyes glittered. "That's right, you'll take me," he said low and hard, "but not before you've had a little taste of what it means to get crosswise of me."

Hastings squeezed his eyes shut and tried to prepare himself for what was to come. He heard Bull start forward on Driver's command.

His plan had gone badly awry.

"Can you handle it?" Wayne asked intently. "Tell me if you don't think so. My life could depend on you backing me up."

"I can do it," Laura said with convincing authority. "I'm to watch the camp from up here. If there's a commotion, then I'm to open fire and keep shooting at the center of the mesa."

Wayne nodded. "That's right. Don't worry about hitting me. I'll be hugging the outer edge. Just keep the lead flying, so Driver's boys will be off balance."

He didn't like having to involve her in a gun battle, and he prayed it wouldn't come to that. But she was the only edge he had in what was going to be a deuced risky business.

"Don't stay in one place," he went on. "Some of those jaspers might be pretty quick in spotting your muzzle flash and firing back. Each time you shoot, move a little bit before you fire again. There's plenty of cover up here."

They were on a rocky ledge above and partway around the curve of the mountain from the small plateau where Driver had established his base.

Reaching it had consumed the early hours of evening. The horses were tied in the woods behind the ledge.

"Once I get clear of the camp with your dad, we'll be headed this way." Wayne didn't mention any of the countless things that could go wrong with his scheme.

Laura gazed silently down through the night at the shadowy outline of the mesa. It was too dark to make out much movement. The carefully banked fire that had been lit after dark had died down and hadn't been replenished. Not even a betraying glow from it was visible. Occasionally Wayne thought he detected a glimmer from under the overhang, where he figured Hastings was confined. Driver wasn't taking any chances on his men being revealed as targets, Wayne figured. But a dark camp made it easier for an enemy to get past the perimeter.

"How are you going to get on the mesa?" Laura asked.

"Driver will have guards out, but I'm betting he won't be expecting an attack from over that ridge. Even if he does have a lookout posted there, he's liable to be careless. Later tonight, when the others are asleep and the guards are drowsy, I'll climb the back wall of the mesa and come up over the ridge."

He'd tried to make it sound like there wasn't any doubt he'd be able to make that climb in the dark. Truth was, he didn't have the foggiest idea if he could do it even in broad daylight. But he couldn't see any other route open.

"It will be dangerous," Laura said, her face pale with worry.

Wayne reached out and embraced her. He sensed in her a need for comfort and reassurance. Her arms encircled him with only a trace of hesitancy, and she buried her face against his shoulder. As he held her and stroked her silky dark tresses, he realized he had needed this as much as she had.

He lost track of time as he held her there, but finally he murmured, "We better get some rest."

He led her to a sheltered space between two boulders. When he seated himself, she sat beside him. With an arm around her shoulders, he held her and watched with heavy eyes as the stars moved slowly overhead.

He could tell by the relaxing of her body when she slept. He allowed himself to sink only into that stage of half-sleep, acquired in the cavalry, wherein his senses would still serve to warn him of any danger.

But nothing threatened, and at last, in the still, small hours of the morning, he drew gently away from her. She made a small sound of protest, then opened her eyes.

"I best be moving out," he said as gently as he could manage.

Even in the poor light he could see the sudden fear and awareness chase the sleep from her lovely features.

She scrambled to her feet as he rose. He felt

her eyes on him as he discarded his Stetson and checked his weapons. He used dust to dull the gleam of the blade of the bowie. When he was finished, she drew close to him.

"Bring him back," she whispered. "You come back, too."

Wayne lifted an open hand and brushed his knuckles along the gentle curve of her jaw. Then he turned and faded into the darkness.

CHAPTER 17

Dark and formidable, the cliff loomed up over him. By craning his neck, he could see its rim edged against the sky a good seventy feet above. Somewhere up there, Wayne was certain, one of Driver's men was pulling guard duty. He hoped the unlikeliness of an assault from this quarter would lull the man into carelessness. He also hoped that he'd be able to climb the cliff without alerting him.

He hitched his shoulders to shift the position of the Winchester. Remembering the awkwardness when he had stalked the bushwhacker earlier, he had taken time to rig a crude rope sling with which to pack the long gun on his back. He would need both hands for this climb. Both hands, and the grace of God, he thought bleakly.

He wished he could have studied the cliff by daylight to pick out a likely route. As it was, he would have to take his chances at finding his way in the darkness as he climbed.

He lifted a booted foot high to step up on an outcrop. By feeling above him for secure holds and testing each with part of his weight before going on, he was able to lift and haul himself up the uneven surface of the cliff.

When he paused to rest his arms and let the sweat cool on his body, he was twenty feet above the ground. After his breathing had quieted a bit, he went on, gripping at the unyielding stone with clawed fingers, pulling himself upward with bulging arms, pushing against precarious footholds with straining legs. The whisper and rustle of his clothing and weapon sheaths sounded unnaturally loud in his ears, as did the ragged draw of his breath. He could see no more than a foot or two in front of him, and dared look upward only at the risk of losing his tenuous grip.

He reached into the black gap of a narrow fissure, groping for a handhold. At the touch of his fingers something inside the fissure moved. Instinctively he snatched his hand back, and for an instant his body swung clear of the cliff, secured there only by the clutch of his other hand and the meager purchase of his toes. The black sky wheeled above him.

With a wrenching effort he thrust his body back against the unyielding stone, clawing for a hold above the ominous mouth of the unnerving fissure. Pebbles skittered away under his fingers with a sound that seemed like that of a landslide. Then he gripped a rocky knob and clung there, heart pounding inside his ribs, sweat cold on his flesh.

As hastily as he could, he inched sideward away from the fissure and its occupant. His fingers found a tough, gnarled plant growing out of an unseen crevice. Gratefully he grasped it and used it to pull himself on up.

Long, straining minutes later, he stopped three feet below the rim to muster his strength. He had no way of knowing what he might be facing when he went up over the edge, but at least he seemed to have made it this far without giving himself away.

At last he extended a seeking hand, found a grip, and drew himself slowly upward until he could peer over the top. For a moment he thought he had given Driver too much credit, that this unlikely route had been left unguarded. Then he made out a shadowy shape seated against a boulder, head tilted forward in the unmistakable droop of a sleeping man. Wayne smiled coldly. Not even Driver's discipline could turn this pack of owlhoots into soldiers.

Hardly daring to breathe, he lifted himself the rest of the way until the reassuring hardness of solid rock was beneath him.

The bowie slid silently from its sheath. Wayne came to his feet in a crouch and crept forward. As he neared the sleeping guard, he chewed the matter over. It would be easiest to kill the fellow, and his death would mean one less enemy. But Wayne didn't take to that kind of killing when he had a choice. If everything went as planned, then he'd have the professor free, and they could be off the mountain well ahead of any pursuit. If things went raw, then he figured what he did to this jasper wouldn't make much difference anyway.

He eased closer. The guard stirred. With a single

movement of his arm, Wayne hit the guard with the hilt of the bowie. The fellow lost consciousness and fell limp.

Wayne left him there and crawled on his belly to the edge of the overhang. He made out slumbering forms scattered about the dead fire. He counted five, which meant two more of them were on the prowl. He needed to locate that pair, but he couldn't afford to take very long in doing it.

One guard would likely be in with the prisoner, and the other would be patrolling the perimeter, he calculated. He delayed long enough to spot the one on patrol trudging away on the far side of the mesa. Then he moved down the sloping ridge to the corner of the overhang's mouth.

Crouched there, he listened. A couple of the sleeping gunslicks were snoring lustily, but he could hear nothing from within the overhang. The snoring helped to cover the sounds of his movements as he rounded the corner and, sinking to one knee, surveyed the shadows beneath the shelf of rock.

The faint gleam of light from the open port of a shielded lantern allowed him to see a haggard Professor Hastings seated slumped against one wall, with a large figure sleeping in front of him like a watchdog.

Wayne crept forward, but the big guard was a light sleeper, or hadn't been asleep at all. He started up with a muttered curse, and Wayne, moving in on him, swung his foot in a savage, lifting arc. The tip of his boot caught the guard's jaw so hard it hurt his toes. The big outlaw dropped, and Wayne, staggering, barely managed to keep from tripping over his inert bulk.

The professor's eyes were open and glittering feverishly in the light of the lantern. Hastings made a hissing sound that carried both relief and satisfaction. Then he twisted over to expose his bound wrists to Wayne's blade. The movement wrenched an involuntary grunt of pain from him.

The honed bowie parted the ropes, and Wayne reached to assist the older man. Hastings flinched at his touch. Wayne frowned as he saw the swelling of his face, evident even in the dim light, and the hunched way he held his body.

"Two ribs broken, I think," Hastings uttered in a harsh whisper.

Wayne felt his fist tighten on the hilt of the bowie. Driver hadn't dealt easy with his prisoner.

"That one did it," the professor's voice was a little louder. He nodded weakly at the senseless guard.

Wayne wished he'd kicked harder. He barely mouthed the words "Can you walk?"

Hasting nodded. "I believe so."

Wayne felt a surge of admiration. Hastings was handling himself like a top hand. He helped the older man to his feet, careful of the busted ribs. Hastings stood like a hunchback. He massaged his forearms with clumsy hands.

As Wayne turned away, Hastings caught his arm and indicated the guard. "Get his gun," he managed.

213

A top hand, for sure, Wayne thought. He'd been on the verge of leaving the outlaw's gun behind.

Hastings took the proffered pistol and stuffed it in his belt. He nodded grimly at Wayne.

With the older man moving in a shuffle behind him, Wayne edged to the mouth of the overhang. He regretted the noise Hastings was making, but in his battered condition, the professor was doing well to be upright at all. Wayne shifted the bowie to his left hand and filled his right with his Colt.

Staying close to the base of the ridge, he led the way toward the edge of the mesa. The snoring from the sleepers continued. None of them moved. Wayne wondered which of them was Driver.

Skirting the rim, with the drop a black void beside them, they worked their way toward the slope that was the only route off the formation.

Behind him, Wayne heard Hastings stumble. Automatically he halted, braced his back, and dropped a shoulder for Hastings to catch and support himself. He had to stiffen his legs under the older man's weight. The professor's harsh breath rasped in his ear. Clumsily Wayne returned the bowie to his sheath, and used that arm to help keep Hastings on his feet.

Hobbling, they made it to the slope. Urgency gripped Wayne. There was still a guard on the prowl, and at any moment one of the sleepers might rouse and sound the alarm.

"Hey! Hold it right there!"

Wayne saw the figure of the patrolling guard forty feet distant along the rim. The outlaw had a rifle and was trying to bring it into play. Wayne's right arm swept up, and the Colt in his hand split the night with lightning. The guard reeled but stayed on his feet. Not a killing shot, Wayne understood, but he had no time for further gunplay.

As he and Hastings lurched down the slope toward the trees at its base, he heard the camp come alive in their wake. Driver's voice shouted questions and commands. A rifle cracked, and a bullet slapped past them.

Where was Laura? he wondered frantically. If she didn't take a hand in this, then both he and the professor were going to wind up dead mighty quick.

The shot from below jolted Laura's nerves, brought her upright, heart pounding. She had been watching the shadowy mesa, straining to pierce the gloom with her eyes. For only a moment she had glanced away, distracted by the sounds of the horses.

Now she could hear yelling from the camp, and another shot exploded. This time she saw the flare of the muzzle flash. Instantly she threw the Winchester to her shoulder and fired, lowered it to work the lever, then lifted it and fired again. There were no targets; she could only follow Wayne's instructions and hope one of her wild shots didn't find him or her father.

Remembering his warning, she moved sideways, dropping to her knees in the shelter of a boulder. Lining the rifle, she fired again. The explosion jarred her ears. Smoke burned her eyes.

She hoped Wayne had reached her father and managed to free him. But even if he had, they must not have gotten clear of the camp. She levered the rifle and pulled the trigger, hardly feeling the kick of the butt against her shoulder. Scrambling a few feet over, she lay flat and sent another bullet winging down into the darkness. The muzzle flash hung before her smoke-teared eyes. She had to blink several times before she could see the mesa again.

Sparks of light flared down there, and she heard the reports of gunfire even over the clamor in her ears. At least some of those shots were directed at her, she realized. The outlaws had spotted her position and were returning fire. Hastily she rolled over, and this time she tried to sight on one of the muzzle flashes before she pulled the trigger.

She kept moving and firing, then cried out in frustration when her rifle ran dry. Dropping the weapon, she fumbled for her father's big Rigby. She had fired it before and dreaded its kick; she had to stand erect to heft it to her shoulder. She fired one barrel, reeled at the impact, then straightened and fired again.

She pulled the little .32 Wayne had insisted she buy back in Heavener. It was no good at this range, she knew, but maybe its bark and flash would keep the outlaws distracted.

Kneeling once more in the protection of the boulder, she emptied it as quickly as she could pull the trigger, then ducked low to reload the

Winchester. A bullet screamed off the boulder. She shivered and tried to ignore the gunfire she was drawing. For a moment she thought she heard shots from higher up the mountain, but guessed it must be only echoes.

With frantic fingers she pushed a final bullet into the Winchester's chamber and levered the rifle to cock it. How much time had gone by? Where were Wayne and her father? Had they been struck by any of the wild shots thrown by herself or the outlaws?

From above bounced the odd echo once again. On the mesa someone screamed. It was an awful sound.

As she propped the rifle barrel atop the rock, she heard more bullets zipping overhead. In the woods behind her, one of the horses gave a shrill, pained whinny. Then there was the sound of hoofbeats.

She lifted the rifle and opened fire again.

She lost track of the bullets she shot but knew she emptied the rifle at least once more. She was trying to load the pistol when a ragged voice called out from the woods. She turned sharply as two stumbling figures lurched into view.

Wayne was half carrying her father, supporting him awkwardly as they clambered the last few steps up the grade. She darted to them.

"Careful, he's hurt," Wayne panted as he lowered the professor.

Hastings sank to his knees but managed to lift a determined look to her. "I'll be fine," he said.

"Go get the horses," Wayne told her. "We need to get out of here. They'll be on our tails, and daylight's not far off." He hesitated, then added, "You did real good. We'd never have made it without you giving us covering fire."

A mixture of pride and relief welled in her as she ran to get the horses. When she reached the grove of saplings where they had left the horses there were only the stubs of broken branches to show where the reins had been secured. Frantic, she ran forward, peering through the gloom, hoping to see the familiar outlines of the beasts.

"What's wrong?" Wayne had followed her.

"They're gone!" she cried, and remembered the pained whinny. "The shooting must've frightened them, so they broke loose. Maybe one of them was creased by a bullet."

For a moment Wayne seemed stricken by the disaster. Then his mouth grew firm, and his eyes narrowed. "Your dad would've had a bad time of it riding, anyway," he said grimly. "We'll have to go to ground." He cast his eyes about. "Somewhere close," he added.

"Perhaps I can help," the professor said. He too had followed her.

Wayne's face mirrored Laura's surprise at the sight of Hastings hobbling forward. He was walking in a stooped fashion, and he had his left arm wrapped protectively around his body. But he seemed to have recovered some from his exhausted condition of only a few moments before.

"What do you mean?" Wayne stepped past her

to address the older man.

"I believe I can lead us to a sanctuary," he announced proudly.

Wayne gaped at him.

"I observed certain landmarks while they were taking me to their hideout," Hastings explained. "I think I know a place that will provide us with concealment. Come on, I'll lead the way."

Hastings wobbled to a halt. The strain of their flight was clearly telling on him, but he managed to lift the walking stick Wayne had cut for him. He used it to point.

"There!" he cried.

Wayne looked past him. They were almost at the top of the mountain. He could see the cloudy morning sky above the trees lining its crest a hundred yards above their position. But Hastings wasn't pointing at the summit. The trembling stick indicated a ledge of rock with a tangled thicket of brush beneath it. Wayne squinted, and something stirred in his memory.

"Come! Come!" Hastings started forward, trying to hurry, only to stumble.

Wayne reached and caught his arm to support him. The professor's face, he saw, was set with a fiery determination that overrode even his pain.

"See?" he panted. "See? I told you." He shrugged free of Wayne's grip and hobbled on.

Wayne lengthened his stride to keep up. Laura was right behind him. Somewhere back down the mountain, he knew, Driver and his men would be looking for them. He had done his hurried best to cover their tracks as they had fled upward, following the pained instructions Hastings had managed to gasp out.

Now, as they halted before the low overhang, Wayne felt his heart begin to pound with something more than the simple exertion of their climb.

"Under there! Behind the brush!" Hastings waved his stick feebly. "It must be there!"

Crouching, Wayne ducked under the ledge. The Winchester was still slung on his back, but he was carrying the Rigby in one hand. He used its twin bores to probe carefully into the brush, remembering the copperhead he glimpsed earlier.

The barrels encountered solid resistance. Wayne knelt and ripped the underbrush aside. He was aware of Hastings and Laura crowding close to the mouth of the small ledge. His eyes widened. He was staring at a stone wall, but not a natural one. The brush hid a crumbling masonry barrier. Some four feet high, it extended the full width of the overhang. In the lower corner to his right, a small hole barely a foot wide gaped blackly at him.

He rocked back on his heels as he realized where Hastings had led them — *Hawken's lost cave.* Before him was undoubtedly the hole through which the mountain man's dog had vanished years ago.

"We must get inside!" Hastings insisted.

Wayne needed no urging. Here was a sanctuary from Driver's pack of wolfhounds. He jammed the butt of the Rigby through the hole and in behind the masonry, then he levered against it hard. He hated to use a good rifle as a prybar, but he had nothing else that would serve.

Sweat popped out on him. In another moment he was sure the rifle butt would crack. Then, faintly, he felt the masonry give. Releasing the rifle, he clamped his fingers on the edge of the hole and heaved backward. It was no good. The wall was about six inches thick, consisting of stone and some kind of mortar. Ages had hardened it.

"Your knife!" Laura had pushed her way in beside him. "Let me have it!"

He fumbled the bowie out and passed it to her. Taking it, she attacked the mortar with its point. Wayne grunted approval, gripped the rifle barrels, and levered hard once more. Some remote part of his mind told him he was the worst kind of greenhorn not to have unloaded the huge gun before putting it to such use.

For frantic moments they labored. Hastings thrust his stick through the shrubs and jabbed impotently at the ancient stonework. Wayne recalled that the wall had withstood the best efforts of a much younger Hawken to breach it with tools such as they were employing against it now.

"It's cracking!" Laura gasped and leaned away.

Wayne sucked air into his lungs and heaved a final time. He stumbled back and almost fell into the brush as a whole four-foot section of masonry gave way. Sharp branches raked Wayne's back. He fought free just as the stale, dusty scent of lost ages rolled out of the chamber behind the wall. Stooping, Wayne peered into blackness.

"Be very careful, Wayne," the professor cautioned. His voice was tight with excitement.

Wayne broke a branch from the closest shrub. He thumb-snapped a lucifer and set it to the leafy stems. Still green, the branch caught and burned with satisfying slowness. Its scent was acrid.

"Give me my knife." He extended his hand without looking around, and felt Laura pass it to him.

Wayne sheathed it and palmed his Colt. Cautiously he ducked through the crumbled wall. He straightened slowly and discovered he had room to lift the makeshift torch. His hand was trembling a little.

The flickering flame illuminated a chamber some twenty feet square and eight feet high. The upper expanses of the walls clearly showed the work of human hands. The far wall looked to be collapsed rubble.

Wayne stepped deeper into the room and stiffened at what he saw. He was barely conscious of Hastings and his daughter following close behind him. He heard both of them suck in their breath sharply.

On a crudely carved stone bier lay a giant armored figure. Torchlight glinted from metal. Wayne moved closer until he was peering down at the bleached features of a grinning helmeted skull. Before him, the armored skeleton of a large man lay in state.

"So here Glome rests," he heard Hastings murmur reverently at his shoulder.

Glome. The Viking chieftain who had led his followers to found a colony in this alien land over a millennium earlier. In this carven tomb his roamings had ended.

Wayne stared down into the empty sockets of the skull and wondered what sort of man this ancient hero had been. The sort Wayne Saddler might have called his pard?

He pulled his gaze away from the skull. All traces of flesh, hair, sinew, and clothing had long since turned to dust, leaving only naked bones in a giant's armor.

A rounded conical helmet with a straight nosepiece protected the skull. A coat of mail lay loosely on the bony breast. On top was an oval piece of metal that might have served as the reinforcement for a wood or leather shield. And resting on the shield, as if still awaiting the clasp of skeletal fingers, was a massive two-edged sword with a tapering blade almost four feet long.

The years and the elements had pitted and corroded the metal so it gleamed only dully in the light of the torch, but still, Wayne knew, the state of preservation was remarkable. The small hole in the wall must have been opened only in fairly recent time. For all those centuries before, the body of Glome had lain sealed in his tomb.

Slowly, almost without volition, Wayne's hand reached for the hilt of the ancient sword. He recognized it as being almost identical to the one he'd unearthed on his farmland. A grip with a rounded pommel and short, down-curving crossguard was affixed to the heavy blade that likely could have hewn through armor such as its owner wore. In a pinch, it could have served to thrust or stab as well.

Wayne's hand hovered, then slowly withdrew. He wouldn't be the one to disturb this long-dead warrior's rest.

Abruptly a shadow darkened the cave mouth at their backs. Wayne spun, lining his gun on the ragged figure just straightening to its full imposing height. For a wild moment Wayne fancied the ghost of Glome himself had risen to confront them.

Then a familiar gravel voice said in tones of awe, "I'll be dadblamed, Pony Soldier. You and your professor and this pretty little gal have managed to find my cave!"

Hawken advanced slowly, gazing about in awe. His two long guns were slung across his back as usual. His approach to the cave mouth must have been all but soundless.

He halted beside the bier and stared at the skeleton. "He one of them Vikings?" he queried at last.

"That's right," Hastings agreed quietly.

Hawken glanced around the chamber again. "Don't see no sign of my pup," he commented sadly.

"There used to be at least one more chamber." Hastings indicated the pile of rubble. "Perhaps your dog was trapped somehow, farther back in the cave, then sealed off by the collapse of the roof. The strata are far from ideal for excavation of a cave. This room was part of a natural overhang that was enlarged. Any additional chambers would be prone to collapse."

Hawken went to stand before the fallen rubble. "Then my pup's somewhere behind all this?"

"His bones, yes," Hastings answered gently. "Along with whatever belongings and possessions of Glome were interred with him. That, I suspect, was the purpose for any additional rooms."

Wayne eyed him speculatively. "You've known the cave was here all along, haven't you, Professor?"

Hastings allowed himself a small smile. "I've known ever since I deciphered the smaller rune stone that Laura uncovered. It was a grave marker for Glome's tomb. Such stones were used fairly often to mark the burial places of Viking chieftains. But this one wasn't placed at the site, for fear the tomb might be despoiled. Rather, it was erected some distance away."

"Those other markings on it were a map," Laura said with dawning comprehension.

Hastings nodded. "A rather cryptic one, I'm afraid, requiring a thorough knowledge of the Germanic Futhark in which it was written. Once I identified certain landmarks, one of which was the blind canyon where the big rune stone was located, I was reasonably certain of being able to locate this site. In fact, I was looking for it when Driver and his men abducted me." He waved an arm about the chamber. "Glome likely had this tomb prepared during his lifetime. When he died, his followers buried him here and moved on. Their fate is likely lost to history, although I would value the opportunity to pursue it." His eyes gleamed as if they were looking on age-old mysteries.

"It's marvelous, Dad," Laura breathed. "This proves all of your theories."

Hastings gave a tight grin of satisfaction. "Yes," he said, "it does."

Wayne turned his gaze on Hawken. "You been dogging our trail?" he asked dryly.

Hawken nodded. "Yep, leastways, I been watching them flatlanders since I seen them come back. I figured they was up to no good. I kept an eye on them." He shrugged ruefully. "Couldn't do much to stop them from laying a lasso on the professor, but I gave you a hand last night when you snuck down into their camp and brung him out, pretty as you please."

Wayne nodded. "I heard you cutting loose with that buffalo gun."

Hawken gave a snort. "I plugged one of them sorry varmints, too. Heard him yell. Sent him to meet his Maker, I reckon."

"I thought your gunshots were echoes!" Laura said in surprise.

"You got one," Wayne still addressed the mountaineer. "I winged another. I figure he's out of action."

Hawken sobered. "That leaves five, unless I've missed count," he calculated.

"That's the way I figure it, too," Wayne agreed. "Couple of them will have headaches."

"They lost your trail already," Hawken advised. "I checked on them before I followed you up here. You know what we got to do, don't you?"

"Yeah." Wayne met the old mountain man's gaze.

Laura looked back and forth between them. "What are you talking about?"

"We can't stay here forever," Wayne explained. "Without Girt as a tracker, they may not be able to trail us here, but that doesn't mean they'll stop looking. Driver's a determined man, and he'll have his back up, now that he's been crossed. Eventually they'll find us. Besides, your dad needs a doc. He may be busted up inside worse than we know. We can't afford to just sit here and wait for them."

"So, what are you going to do?" Laura asked.

"The pony soldier and me are going out to get them backshooters before they get us," Hawken answered for Wayne.

CHAPTER 18

"They done split up," Hawken advised from where he had knelt to study the ground. "Two of them kept going up the mountain — wonder we didn't run into them. The others headed down yonder."

Wayne agreed with the assessment.

Hawken straightened and cast an eye skyward. "Likely to be some rain before the day's out. That'll make tracking them hard."

Wayne looked at the dark, brooding clouds that had been building through the morning and now hung ominously over the mountain. Visibility under the trees would be poor.

"Which ones you want?" Hawken asked. There was a predatory eagerness in his eyes.

"This isn't your fight," Wayne told him.

"Shoot, if it ain't!" Hawken snapped. "This here's my mountain, and I don't cotton to no thieving, murdering valley folk camping out up here and making trouble for my friends!" He stopped of a sudden, as though embarrassed by the admission. "It'd been so long since I'd had much to do with folk, I wasn't sure I liked confabbing with you-all, specially when it made me remember my pup. But I got to pondering on it, and I reckon it wouldn't be so bad to have you-all come up the mountain, now and again, provided I didn't have to parley with you unless I was of a mind to."

It was a lot, coming from the old mountaineer. "We're obliged to you," Wayne told him sincerely.

Hawken dismissed the matter. "Better both of us get cracking. Daylight's burning."

"I'll head after those three downslope," Wayne said. Deliberately he chose the heavier odds for himself, hoping Driver was one of the trio.

"Good enough by me," Hawken said. "Luck to you." Without further amenities he turned and moved away, shrugging the shotgun off his shoulder and into his grip with a single practiced movement. In moments he had disappeared among the trees.

Wayne looked down into the woods below him. On foot, he was going after mounted men, but in parts of this rough terrain that would be to his advantage. He didn't look back as he set out.

Since it was close, he swung by the small mesa, approaching it warily. It was deserted, however, and he found where a lone horseman had ridden slowly away down the mountain. The outlaw who'd caught his bullet last night, he suspected. The fellow was probably cutting his losses and heading to town to find a sawbones to patch him up.

Wayne returned to the trail of his prey. So far, the trio was sticking together. At some point, he calculated, they'd decide that their quarry wasn't ahead of them. Then they'd come back toward the summit, maybe splitting up to cover more territory.

He moved as swiftly as he could, while staying to shelter and keeping a sharp eye out. He was conscious of the fact that the aged Hawken was outnumbered by younger men and that the professor and Laura would be all but helpless back in the cave if the outlaws stumbled upon them. The need for haste spurred him, but if he wasn't careful, he might run smack into the trio he was pursuing.

Crouched on a jutting promontory, he surveyed the mountainside. Dark clouds still brooded overhead. At least there wasn't any sunlight to reflect off metal and betray him to his prey.

He stiffened as movement caught his eye some hundred yards away. In a moment three mounted figures came into view and ascended a barren rocky slope. He squinted, then growled in frustration. Driver wasn't among them.

But he had all three together, and it was a chance he might not have again. This was faster than tracking them down one by one, but it meant he'd be going up against them all at once.

They looked to be on the alert, glancing warily about as they rode. They just weren't looking high enough, Wayne thought.

He lifted the Winchester to his shoulder. Shooting from ambush went against his grain, but there was no other way he and the others could survive against this gang.

He set the sights on the center rider, lifted them a bit, then squeezed the trigger. The echo of the report bounced from the heights behind him. Below, the center rider slewed sideways, then slid limply from his saddle. A killing shot, Wayne assessed darkly.

He levered the Winchester even as he tried to swing it to bear on another target. But both remaining horsemen reacted with the life-and-death reflexes of experienced fighting men. They split into opposite directions, racing their horses into the woods, sparing not so much as a glance at their fallen cohort.

One of them managed to pull his six-gun and fling a wild shot in Wayne's general direction. Wayne tracked that one with his sights and triggered off two fruitless bullets before he disappeared.

Angry with himself, he flung a look after the other one. That one, too, had vanished. Wayne ground his teeth together. He'd lost the element of surprise, with only one fallen foe to show for it. Now they'd be on the lookout for him.

He slipped off the promontory and headed down the grade toward the spot where the six-gun artist had disappeared. Scrambling and sliding, he plunged onward, doing his best to avoid exposing himself in his rapid descent. Once his feet slipped on the decaying leaves, and only an arm hooked around a sturdy sapling kept him from taking a fall.

He slowed his pace only a little. He wanted to

get in close range of his prey before the owlhoot could rightfully expect him to be nearby. He doubted the outlaw would have gone far. He was prey now, too, he reminded himself.

Panting some, he halted in the shelter of a thick oak. He'd last seen his target in about this spot, he estimated. Trying to silence his breathing, he watched and listened. No hoofbeats sounded. Had the outlaw dismounted, or was he working his way uphill in the direction from which Wayne's shot had come?

Like a big mountain cat, Wayne went on. He placed his feet carefully, rifle ready in his hands.

Abruptly the hairs at his nape bristled erect.

"I said you'd never know it, cowboy!" someone called out to him.

Even as the first word was uttered from above him, Wayne was swiveling. He dropped to one knee as he turned, aiming his rifle by sound, even before his eyes focused. A six-gun cracked, and the bullet snapped overhead. Then his sights came into line with the figure throwing down on him from a target-shooting stance. The blast of the rifle merged with the explosion of the revolver. Thirty feet away, the six-gun artist jerked, his arm flying up. Wayne cut loose again. His target's feet slipped from under him, and, on his back, he slid a good ten feet before coming to a loose-limbed halt.

Wayne almost shot him again to be sure. He recognized Hawkface, the man who had tried to trail him from Driver's first camp. Wayne had walked right into his sights. Only the outlaw's boastful need to make himself known had given Wayne a chance to save himself.

He stared down at the body for a long, calculating moment. They were about the same size, he figured. He looked in the direction the final rider had gone. Unless he missed his guess, that one would be headed this way, slow and careful, drawn by the exchange of shots.

Wayne bent over Hawkface's body. Moments later, wearing the dead man's shirt, vest, and hat, he paced forward to meet the final owlhoot. He left his Winchester beside his victim. He moved openly, not trying to stay under cover. He was eager to have this deadly business done.

With his head bowed just a little, he scanned the terrain from under the brim of the Stetson he wore. He found himself straining to catch the sounds of gunfire from farther up the mountain, where Hawken was playing this same sort of stalking game against the other hard cases. Irritated, Wayne pulled his attention back to the matter at hand.

Minutes dragged past as he advanced. Wayne began to wonder if he had miscalculated. Could be the third outlaw was well on his way down the mountain by now, with nary a thought of coming back to side with his compadre.

Then, ahead of him, his eyes picked out a slinking figure. This one, too, was smart enough to have left his horse behind so he'd make a smaller target. Wayne forced himself to continue his seemingly careless progress, although he felt a tingle run the length of his gun arm. He knew he was in plain view of the enemy.

"Jake?" the outlaw called. "Did you plug him?"

Fifty feet away, Wayne estimated. Too far for a sure hit.

"Jake?"

Wayne recognized the voice of Jenner, Driver's young guard.

"Jake, what the devil's the matter with you?"

No more time. Alarm was harsh in Jenner's voice. Wayne slapped the Colt from leather and lifted his head as he thrust his arm out straight for aimed fire. Jenner was fumbling to bring his rifle up. Shock showed clearly on his young face.

The Colt bucked in Wayne's fist. He sighted through the powdersmoke and fired again at Jenner's tottering figure. Jenner's rifle fell to the ground and he dropped in a heap on top of it.

Sucking air, his heart battering against his ribs, Wayne stalked forward, six-gun leveled at the prone form. But he didn't need to shoot again.

A nasty trick to play on a man, Wayne reflected. He shrugged hastily out of the vest and shirt, then sailed the hat aside. Dead man's clothes, he thought with disgust. He needed to collect his own gear and get moving.

He was pivoting away from Jenner's body when the gunfire he had been dreading came rolling down the mountain.

The underbelly of the dark cloud bank hung low above the gloom-shrouded woods. Before the day was out, it was going to become a gullywasher, Hawken reckoned from where he crouched in the concealing brush. He hoped the rain held off until this ugly business was done.

He listened to the approaching horseman. The outlaw was a burly fellow, and Hawken worked his fingers on the familiar haft of his tomahawk in anticipation. He would need to strike sure and fast, and not give the big yahoo a chance to get ahold of him.

He had debated just using his Sharps to pick the target off, but he wanted to keep this silent, so as not to alert Driver, the top dog of the outfit. At the moment, Driver was somewhere on the wooded slope to the east, and he was the more dangerous of the pair. Hawken wanted to reduce the odds before he tangled with the outlaw chieftain.

He had spotted the two riders as they separated to begin a methodical search of this section of the mountain. Given time, Hawken was sure they would discover the cave where the professor and his daughter were lying low. He didn't intend to let that happen.

He had taken great care in stalking the big outlaw, shadowing his course, then finally slipping ahead to conceal himself and lie in wait.

He wondered how Wayne Saddler was faring with the other varmints. He hadn't heard any gunshots, but sometimes sounds carried oddly, or not at all, on the mountain, particularly with the wind sweeping down its face, as it was doing today. He recalled his admission of friendship to the younger man and shook his head in bemusement. He must be getting old *and* soft. Next thing, he'd be hankering to go to church socials and town dances.

The faint rustle of hooves grew closer. Hawken crouched a little lower, tensing himself for the effort. Another moment, and the horse nosed into view. It's rider wore a sullen glower. Hawken saw that his jaw was badly swollen. Likely the big galoot was suffering from a mighty bad headache. Hawken grinned a little. Wayne must have caught him a good lick last night in the camp.

The horse snorted and shuffled sideward a bit. Hawken knew it had picked up his scent. He prayed the beast wouldn't give him away. Angrily the rider sawed at the reins, muttering a curse at his mount. His headache had dulled his senses and put a burr under his saddle, Hawken figured.

He waited until the owlhoot was even with him. Then Hawken surged out of the brush like a puma, slashing the tomahawk around in an arc at the big man's spine while reaching high for the throat with his left hand. The horse was too slow in sidestepping. Hawken felt the tomahawk bite deep. Before his victim could cry out in shock, Hawken had his wiry fingers tangled in the kerchief and shirt at the fellow's throat.

He hauled backward with his whole body, tugging the stricken owlhoot from his saddle. The fellow managed only a croak just before he died.

Hawken made a lunge for the reins. But his hand fell short, and the spooked horse took off like a shot through the darkened forest, heading to the east.

Chest heaving, Hawken watched it go. He was getting old for sure, he told himself bitterly. He could only hope the riderless mount wouldn't be spotted by Driver.

There was no time to waste on regrets. Quickly he freed his tomahawk, then dragged the outlaw's body into the brush. He used a branch to erase the drag marks and signs of the struggle. It wouldn't fool a skilled woodsman, but it would have to do for now.

He slipped the old double-barreled shotgun off his shoulder and glided up the grade. He needed to get to a good vantage point from which he could try to spot Driver. Visibility was poor, but Driver's white duster would make him stand out.

He reached a rugged wall of stone and prepared to clamber up to the ledge at its summit. From the corner of his eye he caught a pale flicker of movement and swung his head in that direction. His muscles went tight. Down the slope a ways to his left, a ghostly white shape seemed to dance in the shadows under the trees.

Driver! Clad in his white duster, which flapped in the wind, the outlaw chief was lurking down there, probably not even aware that he could be seen.

Hawken didn't hesitate. Given another moment, the wily renegade might spot him. He whipped the shotgun to his shoulder and let go both barrels at the phantom white shape below. The twin blast was thunderous. Hawken dropped the shotgun and charged through the cloud of gunsmoke, unlimbering his Sharps as he moved.

Ahead of him he glimpsed the pale, flitting shape. Driver was still on his feet, but Hawken was sure at least a part of the double load of buckshot had gone home. The Sharps would finish the job.

When he had a clear shot through the trees he skidded to a halt and heaved the Sharps up to fire. Then he stared with stupefied shock. Threaded onto a limb, Driver's empty duster capered in the wind. Buckshot had torn the breast of it to tatters.

He'd been fooled, he realized numbly. Warned by the fleeing horse, or maybe having spotted him as he moved, Driver had dangled the duster there to lure him into the open. And he had fallen for it like a famished wolf going after poisoned bait. And his mistake was liable to be just as deadly.

Knowing what to expect, he tried to drop flat, but a mule seemed to kick him in the side, and he heard the flat ugly crack of a rifle from some distance away. He went down, rolled over and over, then scrambled for cover. He'd been hit bad, but it hadn't killed him yet. He heard another shot — the bullet whipped through the leaves overhead.

He pressed a hand to his side and felt the hot wetness there. Driver would be coming to finish him off like a hound after a crippled rabbit, his mind registered dully. The gloom-cloaked woods revolved slowly before his vision, and the darkness edged in numbingly on his senses.

He had to reach shelter so he could make a stand, and he had to protect the professor and his daughter from the human predator who was after them all.

Staggering, his mind spinning in shock, confusion, and pain, Hawken fled up the mountain.

CHAPTER 19

Wayne stared at the frayed, dangling duster with growing horror. The blood on the ground at his feet told the rest of the story. Duped by Driver, Hawken had been lured into his sights. The wound must have been a bad one, because Hawken had left a trail of blood as he took to the woods in flight. Hoofprints showed where Driver had followed him.

Wayne looked up the mountain. He could feel the tautness of his face. He had told Hastings he wanted to be done with battles and showdowns, but that couldn't happen just yet. There was still one more showdown ahead of him.

Turning, he swung up into the saddle of Jenner's horse. He had caught the dead outlaw's mount and ridden it hard as he sought out the site of the gunfire. Now, his fears confirmed, he put heels to the sweating animal and sent it once more up the wooded grade.

The trails were easy to follow. Driver hadn't been in any hurry to overhaul his wounded quarry, and Wayne could only figure that he was hoping Hawken would lead him to the professor. As he rode higher, he realized bleakly that Hawken was doing just that. Wounded, maybe confused or even out of his head, the old mountaineer was headed straight back to the Viking cave.

Wayne pushed the horse harder, confident Driver wouldn't give up his prey now to scout his backtrail for pursuers. He tried to close his mind to the dark imaginings of what might be going on at the cave.

Some distance below the site, he dismounted. Driver and Hawken would already have reached the cave. He'd be a fool to ride in blindly. Best to make the final approach on foot.

Rifle in hand, he slipped warily through the trees. From the edge of the woods he surveyed the overhang carefully. The concealing brush had been torn away and uprooted to reveal the shattered wall. A hint of flickering light within teased his vision.

He forced himself to remain silent and motionless for a few minutes, but he saw no sign of life. Was Driver waiting there in the darkness of the cave? Or, frustrated at failing to find any treasure, had he taken his wrath out on the helpless victims, then gone on his way?

Wayne made a swift, silent run and dropped to a crouch behind what was left of the brush choking the mouth of the overhang. From this angle he couldn't see much beyond the breach in the wall — only the unforgiving darkness with its eerie flickering of light.

Icy centipedes seemed to crawl on the back of his neck. Grim fancies of what might await him in that darkness slithered through his mind like evil serpents. If he wasn't careful, the cave might become a tomb for him as well. He mouthed a silent prayer.

Gently he laid the Winchester aside. Its length would make it awkward to bring into play as he entered the cave. He gripped the Colt and drew a deep steadying breath.

Catlike, gun unsheathed, he eased to the black mouth of the cavern. He stared fruitlessly into the gloom, straining to hear. Only his own shallow breathing reached his ears.

He groped on the ground until his fingers closed on a fragment of the shattered wall. With a short, sharp flick of his wrist, he snapped the fragment into the darkness, then went in fast behind it.

Something silver flashed in the corner of his vision, and a powerful ringing impact wrenched the Colt from his grip. He sprang sideways and turned, crouching, then froze at the spectral scene confronting him.

Saber in fist, teeth bared in a grin as barbaric as that of the Viking skull, Nolen Driver faced him. Behind his menacing figure a makeshift torch flickered from a niche in the wall. By its faint, uncertain light, he could make out three still forms against the wall. Laura and her father were bound and gagged. Hawken was curled like a wounded varmint in the corner. Dead or alive, Wayne couldn't tell.

Driver's chuckle echoed sepulchrally. The tip of his sword made little dancing motions. "I did the same thing to the professor there," he boasted.

"Two for two. Not bad for going up against a six-gun with a sword. But don't get any ideas!" Deftly, he tossed the saber from right hand to left and pulled his Colt. He gave that unholy chuckle again.

"I figured you'd be coming, Saddler, so I just made your friends nice and comfortable and then settled back to wait." He gestured with the sword. "That old coot, whoever he is, did in Bull with a blasted tomahawk, but I used a little tactical diversion on him, and when he fell for it, I plugged him. He's the one who led me here."

Over Driver's shoulder Wayne could see the pale mask of Laura's face. Her eyes were wide, and even in the gloom he could read the fear in their depths.

"Bull's not the only one done for," Wayne said softly. "Your whole command's gone, Driver. Wiped out to a man."

Anger twisted Driver's mouth, then vanished. "But you're the one who's a prisoner," he gloated. "And I won't be needing another command, now that I've got what I was after."

"What's that?" Wayne demanded flatly.

"The treasure! The Viking treasure!"

"Look around you, man! There's no treasure here!"

"Don't play me for a tenderfoot," Driver advised coldly. Again he used the saber as a pointer. "You think I don't know what's behind that rubble? Another chamber. That's where the gold is!"

"You're loco, Driver. Even if there was any gold behind all that, how do you think you're going to get it out?"

"I'll blast it out. I've got me a couple of sticks of dynamite that ought to do the job real nice."

"You'll bring the whole cave down!"

Driver shook his head confidently. "Why do you think I kept the professor alive? He's an expert on excavating places like this. He'll tell me how to set it, and if he doesn't, well, I reckon I can use his pretty little girl to help him rethink his decision."

"An officer and a gentleman," Wayne said dryly.

Driver stiffened. "I don't make war on women! If anything happens to the girl, it's your and the professor's doing, not mine. I knew you and I were liable to butt heads from the first, so I offered you a place in my command. But you were too stubborn to listen. Well, now the dust has settled, and the field is mine!"

Wayne eyed him carefully. There was no way to get past the twin threats of the menacing blade and the leveled gun. Driver was right; he was in command of this battlefield.

Then, in the far corner, just out of the range of Driver's vision, the huddled shape that was Hawken moved. Slowly, like a revenant rising from a grave, the old mountaineer sat up.

Wayne's throat was dry. He tried not to let a thing show on his face. "What are your plans for me?" Wayne asked, because he had to keep Driver talking.

Driver made a little parrying movement with the sword. Even left-handed, he had some skill. "Like I said, I figured you'd be coming back here, so I just sat tight and waited. Saw you come sneaking up out of the woods. You moved real good."

Sitting up, left hand pressed to his side, Hawken groped in the shadows beside him and came up with a long, straight object — the professor's crude walking stick.

"You're wondering why I let you live," Driver went on. "I could've shot you down outside, or put this blade through you when you entered. But that wouldn't have been proper military procedure. I wanted to accept your surrender — one soldier to another."

Awkwardly Hawken lifted the stick. He drew his right arm back like an Indian getting set to hurl his lance. The stick wobbled in his grip.

"You're no soldier," Wayne said coldly. "You're a thief and a murderer. If you were in my command, I'd cashier you before you had time to come to attention."

Ferocity writhed across Driver's face. With a single violent movement of his arm, he thrust the Colt at Wayne's chest, hammer back.

Hawken's arm snapped forward. The walking stick hurtled through the dim light and struck the gun in Driver's hand with unerring accuracy. Stick and gun clattered to the stone. Driver snarled with shock and anger. Hawken collapsed limply as Wayne lunged for Driver's throat.

But even though taken by surprise, Driver tossed the saber from one hand to the other. His right took the hilt, and he extended his arm in a simple thrust that almost impaled Wayne coming in.

Wayne pulled up short, twisting his upper body aside. Driver grinned with savagery, lifted the saber, looped it around, and stepped forward with a sweeping slash at Wayne's neck. Wayne ducked, felt the blade shear the Stetson from his head. Driver rotated his wrist and cut backhanded in followup.

Helplessly Wayne flung himself away. His spine fetched up bruisingly against the stone bier. Driver sneered exultantly and brought the saber down from overhead. Wayne's outflung hand brushed over bone and metal. His fingers touched the hilt of the ancient Viking sword and closed desperately about it. With an arm-wrenching effort he heaved the weapon up to block Driver's descending blade.

New steel clashed against ancient, and echoes rang in the tomb. Driver's eyes widened. Braced against the bier, Wayne lifted a booted foot and lashed out. Driver lurched back, caught himself, and fell into his sideward fencing stance — knees bent, right foot pointed forward, left foot at an angle, right arm crooked, with saber at ready. Wayne shifted his own feet into the same familiar stance, and swung the heavy Viking blade to a guard position.

About to attack again, Driver halted. "It's better this way," he enthused with wicked satisfaction.

"Now we'll see who's the better man with cold steel!"

"On guard!" Wayne barked and uncoiled with a savage slash.

The Viking blade was no tool for fencing, he realized immediately, but, in that heady moment, it didn't matter. The sword was a bladed weapon meant for killing, and he had it in his fist. He could ask for nothing more.

Driver parried the slash neatly, pressed the heavier blade down with his own, and came in over it, smooth and fast, as if giving a demonstration at a cavalry fencing tournament. Awkwardly, because of its unaccustomed weight, Wayne circled the big blade up and around to batter Driver's saber aside. He faded away from the bier to find room as Driver came at him like a berserker.

There was not time to mount an offense. It took every ounce of Wayne's skill and speed to keep Driver's darting, lunging, slashing saber from his flesh. He felt as though he were dueling with a windmill. Driver came over the old blade, then under it, then attacked it like a smith beating on an anvil. All the strength of Wayne's wrist and arm went into manipulating the Viking weapon. He hadn't faced another swordsman in years, and never one as skilled as Driver.

He backstepped, keeping his stance, shifting the heavy blade from side to side, circling it to disengage, dropping it to block, raising it to meet savage cuts at skull and neck and shoulder. The clamor of metal on metal rang and gonged and belled from the ancient stone.

Wayne sensed the wall close behind him, blocking any further retreat. He flexed his legs and leapt sideways. Driver's lunging blade darted past his side and scarred the stone. Wayne hewed down at Driver as if he were trying to cleave armor — the kind of crashing blow for which the Viking blade had been forged. Driver snapped his extended body back like a snake recoiling, and swung the saber up to meet the cut. Sparks flared at the contact, and the weight of the Norse weapon bore the lighter saber down. Then the bigger blade slid off to the side with a rasp of steel, and Driver slashed a backhanded stroke in return.

Wayne got the Viking blade in place to counter it, but he stumbled and almost fell as he wheeled clear. His breath was beginning to tear at his lungs, and he was having trouble following the movements of the saber in the dim light. He had a moment's view of Laura's ghostly, horrified face.

Driver stamped and swept in with a slash, the saber like an extension of his arm. Wayne parried and gave ground. Something turned beneath his foot — one of the discarded six-guns. His rear leg buckled, and talons of fear gripped him as he felt himself going down.

His shoulders jarred against the hard stone of the floor. Laughing, Driver towered above him like some pagan warrior of old. The saber slashed down — and struck sparks from the rock as Wayne rolled aside. He came up on one knee, sweeping the Norse blade in an arc that struck nothing but held Driver at bay until Wayne could get his feet under him.

Clear of the big sword's range, Driver saluted mockingly with his saber. He was breathing hard himself, but his smile was as cold as the steel of his sword.

"You're good, Saddler, I don't think I've ever faced better."

Wayne lifted the big sword to present its point, although his arm and shoulder throbbed under its weight. "This isn't a post tournament or a duel against some greenhorn lieutenant," he gibed.

With the last word, he beat Driver's offered blade wide, and lunged, sword arm extended, left leg out straight behind him. The Viking sword wasn't meant for that sort of technique. He prayed Driver wouldn't be ready for it. But Driver was. He worked his wrist in a circular disengage, and lunged in turn. Steel screeched along steel as their blades rasped together. They came hilt to hilt and face to face, straining against each other. Driver's eyes were those of a demon. He jerked a knee up at Wayne's groin. Expecting it, Wayne turned a thigh to block. He hooked his foot behind Driver's anchor leg and threw a shoulder into his chest. Off balance, Driver staggered back, and Wayne sprang after and slashed.

Driver's entire arm and shoulder went into the sweeping upward parry he executed. Steel clashed discordantly, and the shock traveled down

Wayne's arm. The old Viking blade, weakened by the centuries and battering it had taken in the last few minutes, snapped off clean, six inches above the hilt.

Wayne skipped backward. Surprise froze Driver for a piece of a second. Then he hissed in victory and shifted his feet to come in for the kill.

Wayne threw the hilt from right hand to left and ripped the bowie from its sheath as Driver slashed down at his skull. The hewing blade of the saber crashed into the V of the crossed hilt and bowie knife that Wayne thrust up to meet it. He flexed his wrist to catch the saber between the down-curving guard of the hilt and what was left of the Viking blade. In the instant the saber was locked, he brought his right arm down and drove the bowie into Driver's body.

Driver took a tottering step back. Wayne pulled the knife free. Driver's face was white with shock. The saber clanged to the floor. His feet carried him uncertainly backward almost to the collapsed pile of rubble, and he sank to his knees.

Panting, Wayne moved closer, bowie still in his fist.

Driver lifted his head to stare up at him from agonized eyes. Then he fell on his side and lay still.

If any man is killed, I'll make him a corporal, Wayne thought bleakly.

He came about. On unsteady legs he crossed to the prisoners and sawed at their bonds with the bowie. Her hands free, Laura snatched the gag from her mouth.

"Oh, thank God!" she cried hoarsely, and folded her arms about him.

He held her for a moment, then turned and freed her father.

"Wayne!" Laura's scream bounced echoes. "He's not dead!"

Wayne whirled in a crouch. Still crumpled against the wall of rubble, Driver leered up at him with a visage of purest evil. In one hand was a red cylinder. In the other was a flaming match, which he applied shakily to the cylinder's fuse.

"I'll have my gold, and take you with me, Saddler!"

"Dynamite! Get out!" Wayne roared.

He sensed Laura and the professor scrambling for the mouth of the cave as he whirled to scoop Hawken's limp form up in his arms. Driver's maniacal laughter rang behind him as he thrust Hawken through the breached wall into the waiting hands of the pair outside. He heaved himself out through the aperture.

"Go on! Run!" he shouted.

Once more he caught Hawken up like a child and raced for the shelter of the trees. The blast hit him from behind like the slap of a great flaming hand. Stone and gravel and shards of masonry pelted him. As he was flung forward, he dropped Hawken, fetching up just at the edge of the woods. Dazedly he looked back where the cave had been.

The overhang and the cavern mouth were gone, obliterated under a pile of stone and debris. A cloud of dust rolled chokingly over him.

Laura and Hastings were picking themselves up on either side of him. Laura scrambled to Hawken on hands and knees.

"He's still alive!" she exclaimed after a moment.

Wayne exhaled a sigh of relief. He glanced over at Hastings.

The professor was staring with a haunted expression at the mound of stone debris. "I hope he found his gold," he said bitterly.

Wayne regarded him. "Was there ever any gold, Professor?"

Hastings turned bleak eyes on him. "Who can say? But there *was* another chamber to the tomb. Presumably it held Glome's most prized possessions and belongings. His settlement was an isolated enclave. There's no way of knowing what practices or customs they might've developed. Perhaps they buried whatever treasure Glome had, along with him. We'll never know for sure."

Wayne blinked against the dust. So maybe Driver had been right, after all. Maybe he was entombed now with his gold. Wayne sketched a half-hearted salute at the buried cave, then let his arm fall tiredly to his side.

He felt the first drops of cold, cleansing rain strike his bare head.

CHAPTER 20

"Heard about the ruckus, and figured I better check on things before I hitched up with Madsen and Tilghman," Heck Thomas said. "But sounds like you had everything in hand. I was right — you're just as good as you were in the old days."

Wayne frowned. He was going to have nightmare recollections of Nolen Driver's flashing blade for a long spell to come. "It was a bearcat, Heck," he confessed.

The graying lawman smiled thinly. "Nothing you couldn't handle." He looked at Wayne and Laura, who shared the table with him in Heavener's café. "And you two came through it all fat and sassy." He sobered. "How's the old mountain man?"

"The doc says he'll be back on his feet before too long." Now Wayne smiled, too, remembering Hawken's protestations upon recovering consciousness and finding he'd been hauled down to civilization against his will. "And, unless I miss my guess, it will be a lot sooner than the doc expects. Hawken's already raring to get back up the mountain."

Heck shook his head wonderingly. "An honest-to-goodness mountain man in this day and age.

I want to meet him before I leave."

"You'll take a liking to him," Wayne predicted. He hoped he'd be present when those two aging warriors met.

"And what about your father, Miss Laura?" Heck queried. "Is he recovering?"

She nodded with a brief smile. "And he's almost as eager as Hawken to get back on the mountain and continue his research," she added.

"So he hasn't given up, after having the Viking tomb destroyed?"

Laura gave a quick shake of her head. "Oh, no, not Dad. He was upset, of course, but, after all, he still has the rune stones, and he's certain there must be more artifacts left behind by Glome's followers. He's even planning on bringing out some more assistants. He's sure the university will permit it, on the basis of our finds."

"And do you plan on continuing as one of his assistants?"

Laura's eyes darted sideways in Wayne's direction. She ducked her head, and a blush crept up her neck. "Why, yes, I suppose," she stammered.

Heck eyed the pair of them for a shrewd moment. Then he grinned. "You did a fine job, Wayne. The Territory's well rid of Driver and his pack. Sorry if I threw you to the wolves, but I didn't reckon on you having to take on that whole bunch."

"I had some help."

"So you've told me." Heck's grin turned mischievous. "Sounds like you and Miss Laura made quite a team." He appreciated their reactions for a moment before continuing in a more serious tone. "You ought to give some thought to pinning on a badge again, Wayne. Oklahoma needs lawmen like you."

"It needs farmers, too." Wayne was aware of Laura's eyes resting briefly on him. "And I figure to get me a few head of horses and some cattle, maybe try my hand at a little ranching, as well. There'll come a day, before too long, when farmers and ranchers are more important to Oklahoma than peace officers."

Heck sighed with a tinge of what might have been regret. "I expect you're right. Won't be much left for an old warhorse like me except the pasture."

"You've still got Doolin and his gang to worry about," Wayne reminded him.

Heck snorted. "Yeah, there's still Doolin," he agreed, pushing back his chair. "I got a bit more business here in town, then I'd appreciate an introduction to your mountaineer."

"Done." Wayne stood and gripped his hand.

Heck's grin turned sly once more. "And, unless I'm reading the cards all wrong, the two of you have some business to tend to, as well. Miss Laura." He touched a forefinger to the brim of his hat and, turning, ambled out of the café.

Wayne sat down. Laura was blushing a fierce crimson and didn't meet his gaze. He glanced about. The small, balding proprietor had disappeared in the back. They had the café to themselves. Time for a showdown of a different type, he thought.

He became aware that Laura had turned a timid gaze on him. Awkwardly he reached across the table for one of her hands, and felt a thrill as her fingers entwined eagerly with his. But her eyes were still evasive.

"You heard what I said to Heck," he began.

Laura's head came up with the firmness of sudden resolution. "Wait, Wayne," she forestalled him. "I have to tell you something. I — I want to apologize."

"What?" Wayne said in surprise.

"I didn't want to be mean to you," she rushed on, "but, first Dad said some things, and then, too, I was scared."

"Scared of me?" Wayne asked in puzzlement.

"No, no, not scared of you." Tears filled her eyes. "I was scared of myself. Scared of not knowing what to say or do around you, scared that I'd do the wrong thing and lose you." Her fingers tightened around his. "I've never had too much to do with men, and I knew you must've had lots of lady friends. I was terrified that, next to them, you'd think I was silly and foolish and childish."

Wayne tried to speak, but she wouldn't be cut off. "Then, when Driver took us prisoner, and he was waiting there to kill you, and I knew he'd kill us, too, I realized there were worse things to be scared of, things like losing you because I was too afraid of making a fool of myself to ever let you know that I cared about you."

256

Wayne touched a silencing finger to her lips. "There's never been anyone else like you in my life, and that scares me a little bit, too. I've never been in love before."

She caught her breath sharply at his words.

"Listen to me," he continued. "There's nothing you could do that would run me off, not now, not ever. If we just follow our hearts, and our morals, and our common sense, we'll do just fine. I love you, Laura. I want you to be my bride." He managed a grin. "Even if the prospect scares you to death!"

"It doesn't scare me at all, now," she whispered.

He was on his feet and around the table to her in a stride. She came easily into his arms, and this time there was nothing fleeting or hesitant about the press of her lips against his.

When at last she leaned back in the circle of his arms, he grinned down at her ruefully. "I guess I still need to get your father's consent."

Her answering smile carried a hidden knowledge. "That's all right," she said with assurance. "I think you already have it."

The employees of G.K. HALL hope you have enjoyed this Large Print book. All our Large Print titles are designed for easy reading, and all our books are made to last. Other G.K. Hall Large Print books are available at your library, through selected bookstores, or directly from us. For more information about current and upcoming titles, please call or mail your name and address to:

G.K. HALL
PO Box 159
Thorndike, Maine 04986
800/223-6121
207/948-2962